**the first paper girl
in red oak,
iowa**

the first paper girl

in red oak,

iowa

AND

OTHER

STORIES

11-5-05

For Carol:
With warm
regards,

Elizabeth SF

~~Elizabeth Stuckey-French~~

Doubleday

New York   London   Toronto   Sydney   Auckland

PUBLISHED BY DOUBLEDAY
a division of Random House, Inc.
1540 Broadway, New York, New York 10036

DOUBLEDAY and the portrayal of an anchor with a dolphin are
trademarks of Doubleday, a division of Random House, Inc.

Book design by Judith Stagnitto Abbate

Library of Congress Cataloging-in-Publication Data

Stuckey-French, Elizabeth.
    The first paper girl in Red Oak, Iowa, and other
    stories/by Elizabeth Stuckey-French.— 1st ed.
        p. cm.
    Contents: Junior—Doodlebug—The first paper girl in
Red Oak, Iowa—Famous poets—Blessing—Plywood
rabbit—Scavenger hunt—Search and rescue—Leufredus—
Professor claims he found formula for ancient steel—
Electric wizard—The visible man.
    1. Middle West—Social life and customs—Fiction.
I. Title: First paper girl in Red Oak, Iowa. II. Title.

PS3569.T832 F5 2000
813'.6—dc21   99-086606

ISBN 0-385-49893-4

Printed in the United States of America

June 2000

First Edition

10 9 8 7 6 5 4 3 2 1

The following stories have previously appeared and are
reprinted by permission of the author:

"Junior," *The Atlantic Monthly*, April 1996

"Doodlebug," *Cottonwood*, Summer 1995

"The First Paper Girl in Red Oak, Iowa,"
    the *Gettysburg Review*, Winter 1998

"Famous Poets," *Arts Indiana*, 1990

"Blessing," *Indiannual 4*, 1988, and
    New Territory: Contemporary Indiana Fiction,
    1990

"Plywood Rabbit," *Arts Indiana*, 1988,
    reprinted in the *Indianapolis Star*,
    October 8, 1989

"Scavenger Hunt," the *Washington Square Press*,
    Spring 2000

"Search and Rescue," *Indiannual 8*, 1992

"Leufredus," the *Southern Review*,
    Autumn 1998

"Electric Wizard," *The Atlantic Monthly*,
    June 1998

For Ned, Flannery, and Phoebe

AcknoWledgments

I am grateful for the James Michener–Paul Engle Fellowship and the Indiana Artist Grant, which allowed me to complete this collection. For their kindness and hard work I wish to thank C. Michael Curtis, Gail Hochman, Deb Futter, and Marianne Merola. I couldn't have done it without the wise counsel and friendship of the Creative Girls: Eileen Bartos, Mo Jones, Suzanne Kelsey, Jane Olson, Tonja Robins, Mary Helen Stefaniak, Mary Vermillion, and Ann Zerkel. Thanks to Brian and Helen Feltovitch, Jacinta Hart, Alison (Sister) Jester, C. Elizabeth Perry, M.D., Natalia Singer, Amy Peters and Peter Sims, and the late Jerome Donahue for lighting up my stories and my life. I am indebted to my teachers—Liz Inness-Brown, Patricia Henley, Francine Prose, Ethan Canin, and Frank Conroy—and to Connie Brothers and Karen Thielman for their generosity and encouragement. My endless gratitude goes to

my parents, who taught me to love reading and writing stories. Most of all I thank my husband, Ned, for everything
and then some.

This book is also dedicated to the memory of Paige
Barnett.

Contents

Contents

Like most people, she never really believed
that one terrible thing would happen after another.

Two Serious Ladies—**Jane Bowles**

the first paper girl
in red oak,
iowa

Junior

THE CITY pool was full of children that day, but I don't think that's what bothered me. I was fourteen and happy to be out with my friends. It was sunny but cool for mid-July in Iowa. A breeze flipped up the edges of our beach towels as we lined them up on the crumbling cement, anchoring them with clogs, a bottle of coconut oil, and a transistor radio which seemed to play nothing but Sammy Davis, Jr., singing "The Candy Man." My friends flopped down on their backs and fell asleep, but I couldn't relax. I sat cross-legged in my faded bikini, a hand-me-down from my sister Daisy.

Daisy was lifeguarding, but she couldn't see me, didn't even know I was there. She looked like a stranger perched above the masses in her red tank suit and mirror sunglasses, her nose a triangle of zinc oxide. In one month, she was going away to college, leaving me to take care of our father. I couldn't let myself think about how dreary life would be without Daisy. I gazed out at the pool, which was circular, with the deep part and diving island in the center. A group of four or five children splashed around at the edge of the deep water, shrieking and dunking each other. A smaller girl in a green one-piece bathing suit dog-paddled near the splashers, barely keeping her chin above water. She wanted to play too, but the other children—friends? neighbors? sisters and brothers?—ignored her. Teenagers were doing cannonballs off the high dive, and their waves sloshed over her head. Nobody except me seemed to notice. The girl was paddling as hard as she could, getting nowhere.

I stood up and waded into the water, which reeked of chlorine, and began swimming the breaststroke toward the group of children, holding my head up as a snake does. The older kids moved off toward the slide, leaving the little girl behind. When she saw me, she opened her eyes wide and reached out. I didn't have a clue how to rescue someone. I took her hand and she clawed her way up my arm. She was on me like a monkey. Her legs swung up and wrapped around my neck, dunking me, choking me. I tried to stand, but I couldn't touch bottom. She kicked me, hard, in the jaw. I shoved her away but she held on to me. I'd had enough of this kind of treatment. My hand gripped her head like a rubber ball. I held her underwater and watched her thin body squirming in its green ruffled suit.

Someone finally screamed, and the lifeguards began blowing their whistles. Daisy dove from her chair in a red flash. Still I held the girl under. It's too late now, was the only thought I remember having. A man tackled me from behind, and Daisy jerked the girl from the water. The man gripped me tightly to his blubbery chest, as if I were trying to run away. Over on the cement Daisy knelt beside the girl and gave her mouth-to-mouth. After a few seconds Daisy stood up, holding the squalling girl, stroking her wet hair. The ruffles on the girl's suit were flipped up and plastered to her body. "Daisy," I called out. When Daisy looked over at me, her face slack with shock, I realized what I'd done.

Everything after that seemed nightmarish but inevitable. Daisy and I were taken up to the pool manager's office, dripping wet, to sit in plastic chairs and wait for the police. The detective who came wore a velour shirt and looked familiar, like someone I might've seen at church. Daisy reported what had happened in a businesslike voice, while I stared at the tufts of hair on my big toes, wondering if I should shave them. The detective asked me if I had anything to add. "She tried to drown me first," I said.

"That's not how the witnesses tell it," he said.

I glanced over at Daisy. "Sorry," she said, ever the honest one. "I didn't see that part."

At my hearing, we sat on a bench in front of the juvenile judge—first the detective, then my father, hanging his head, then my sister Daisy, her arm around my father, and then me. My mother, who'd washed her hands of us, didn't show. Because of my previous record—shoplifting and truancy—the judge decided to send me to the Cary Home in Des Moines for one school year.

The Cary Home for Girls was an elegant brick house tucked into a cul-de-sac on the edge of an upper-class neighborhood. From the outside, you'd never know it contained six teenage delinquents and their live-in counselors. We bad girls attended class in the large attic of the house, ate pizza burgers, did homework together, and watched reruns of "The Dick Van Dyke Show." It hardly felt like punishment.

At night, though, things fell apart. I had relentless dreams about Lisa Lazar, the little girl from the pool. She came to the Cary Home in her ruffled bathing suit and invited me outside to play. When she smiled, crooking her finger at me, I woke up terrified. I would stare at the buzzing streetlight outside my bedroom window and wonder what someone like me was doing at the Cary Home, someone who, until recently, had played by the rules, was fairly popular, had a semi-cute boyfriend, and tried her best to get decent grades.

In April, near the end of my stay at Cary Home, my father called to tell me that his sister, Marie-Therese, was coming to see me. "She wants to help out," he said. I'd never met my aunt before. She and my father exchanged Christmas cards and birthday phone calls, but that was about it. "Marie stays on the move. She's a wheeler-dealer," was my father's only explanation of why we never saw her. I wasn't sure what a wheeler-dealer was, but it sounded intriguing.

On the evening of her visit, I stepped into the living room and saw a fattish woman in baggy shorts and huiraches sprawled on the sofa, snoring. I recognized her dark curly hair and sharp features from an old photo I'd once found in my father's desk at the *Magruder Times*, of which he was the editor—a photo of my father and Marie-Therese as children, posing in chaps and cowboy boots in front of some mountains in New Mexico, where they grew up. I said, "Hello?"

She bounced up, wide awake. "I'm your aunt Merry," she said, shaking my hand. "M-E-R-R-Y, as in Christmas."

We sat down across from each other and she explained that she'd recently changed her name to Merry because she'd moved to Columbus, Ohio. "Midwesterners don't like anything Frenchy," she said.

"That's true," I said. I was disappointed that she'd changed her name and looked so ordinary and lived in Ohio. Out of the corner of my eye, I saw my roommate, the klepto, in the yard, peering in through the screen window. She was sneaking out to meet her boyfriend the arsonist. She bugged out her eyes and flicked her tongue. I ignored her. I asked Merry, "Why'd you decide to come see me?"

"Brother said family could visit," she said. "And I'm family, last I checked."

"Thanks," I said. My parents had never once been to see

me at the home. My father was too ashamed, and my mother was too busy looking after her own father, Smitty, who owned the *Times*. Daisy, who'd postponed college for a year, drove over every Sunday and took me out to the movies or the Frozen Custard. We always got teary when we said good-bye. She would ruffle my hair and call me Squirt, willing me to be innocent again.

"Listen, sugar," said Merry, leaning forward with her elbows on her knees. "I called Brother last week 'cause I got the feeling something was wrong. He's worried sick. I offered to look after you, just for the summer. Transitional period. Before you go home."

So they didn't want me back. "I committed a crime," I said. "That's why I'm here."

"Nice place, too." Merry looked around at our cozy living room, furnished in Early American sofas and chairs that could swallow you whole.

"I don't want to be in the way," I said. "Don't you have a family in Ohio?" I knew she'd been married twice and had step-children.

"Oh, sure," she said. "But we won't be going to Ohio. We'll be staying out at the homeplace, in New Mexico."

My father once wrote a piece for the newspaper about what it was like to grow up on a ranch—haying, feeding livestock, planting and watering alfalfa—but he never talked to us about New Mexico. His parents had been to visit us a few times when I was little, but I barely remembered them. Now his father was dead and his mother was a sick old lady. "Why do we have to go out there?" I asked Merry.

She took my hand and squeezed it. One of her eyes was blue, the other green. "I'm a psychic," she said. "You're going to be helping me with a job. Mom has offered us the use of her home."

"I tried to kill someone," I said. "A small child."

"I know, sugar," Merry said. "You did an extremely vicious

thing." She stood up and slung her purse strap over her shoulder, as if that settled that.

I was relieved, if only for a moment, to think that it did.

Aunt Merry and I left for New Mexico the last week of June. In Kansas she insisted that I drive her Lincoln Continental. I had my learner's permit, but I'd never driven on the interstate.

"Don't sweat it," Merry said. "The Queen Mary handles like a dream."

I sat up straight, my hands gripping the wheel as we rolled across Kansas at 70 miles per hour. Merry propped her bare feet up on the dashboard, knees tucked under her purple caftan. If I dropped down to 65, she would bark out, "What are you waiting for? A tow?" If I sped up to 75, she'd imitate a police siren.

But most of the time she talked about herself. "I wear different-colored contacts," she said. "Throws people off balance. They pop out sometimes, but I always find them. I have ESP. Had it since I was a kid. Once Brother lost his G-Man ring and I led him right to the spot, in the schoolyard, where it fell off his finger. Unfortunately, someone had stepped on it by then. When I was your age, Mom put me on the radio. My own psychic call-in show. I directed a woman right to where her baby wandered off to—the bottom of a well. Brother was so jealous."

I didn't want to reveal how eager I was to learn anything about my father. "Was he?" I said in a neutral tone.

"He was," Merry said. "He got stuck with all the chores. Didn't stand up for himself. Held it all in, till he couldn't take it anymore." She started humming "Rock of Ages" and stared out the window, letting me know she was finished with that subject.

We passed a muddy lot packed tight with cattle that seemed to go on for miles, bigger than anything I'd ever seen in Iowa. Finally I asked Merry, "Do you still have a radio show?"

"Oh no, but I still help people find things. They call me up from all over the U.S. and Canada. Missing dogs are my specialty." She studied her feet and wiggled her red-painted toes.

Merry was more childlike, and more self-confident, than any adult I'd ever known. She didn't seem to realize, or care, how weird she was. I said, "How do you find missing dogs?" Up ahead, in my lane, a station wagon was going much too slow.

"Pass him, pass him!" Merry yelled. We surged around the station wagon and veered back into our own lane. Merry went on in her ordinary voice, "Say, for example, some rich guy calls me from Indiana. He and his wife are missing their yellow Lab, Captain Crunch. Someone stole him right out of his pen. Man and his wife are distraught. Dog's a kid substitute. They've been offering a two-thousand-dollar reward, but no leads. I'm quiet for a while, and then I say, 'Your dog is safe. I see a late-model Ford, dark green, with two men in it. They drag Captain Crunch into their car. I see them driving to New Mexico. They're taking the dog to Los Alamos, for research purposes. But they stop at a convenience store in Española, and the Captain escapes.'

" 'Thank God,' says the man. 'Where is he now?'

" 'I can't tell exactly,' I say. 'Put an ad in the *Santa Fe New Mexican*. You'll find him.'

"He says, 'Thank you, thank you' and says he'll send me a check for my commission."

"Are you right all the time?" I felt as if Aunt Merry and I were aliens, flying through the wheat fields in a space ship.

"One hundred percent of the time." She swiveled to face me, the gold trim around the neck of her caftan glittering. "I can guarantee that somebody living with her grandmother just outside Santa Fe will answer that ad, and the happy couple will drive to New Mexico to pick up their dog. My little helper will hand over most of the reward money to me, keeping a bit for herself. All the time I'll be back in Ohio, so nobody can connect us. Not that these people ever try. They might suspect they've been had, but they've got a new dog. Everyone's happy. Even the dog."

I glanced down at the pavement racing underneath us. "I thought you had a gift."

"I do," she said. "I know how to make a living."

"I'm getting tired," I said. "My eyes aren't seeing very well."

"At the next rest area, pull over and take five."

"What if you can't find a dog that looks like theirs?"

"He's waiting at Mother's. Captain Crunch Junior." She swung her feet back up on the dashboard. "It'll be an adventure, sugar," she said.

My grandmother lived in a low brick house with tiny windows, surrounded by ramshackle outbuildings that looked like they were floating in a sea of red dirt. A few cottonwood trees punctuated the gray-green sagebrush. "This is a farm?" I asked Merry. "I thought you lived on a farm."

"We utilized an irrigation system," Merry said.

When we got out of the car, I saw a dog tied to the corner-post of the front porch. He was yellow, but he looked part Lab and part something else. He was smaller than a Lab and had floppy ears. "They'll never believe this is their dog," I said. He strained at the rope and wagged his tail. "Is that the best you could find?"

"Now don't speak ill of our canine friend," Merry said. She took the two bags of groceries we'd just purchased out of the trunk of her car and thrust them into my arms. Then she leaned further into the trunk and emerged with a small TV set.

"What's that for?" I said.

"For you," she said, and grinned. Her teeth were too white.

Inside, while Merry unpacked the groceries, I wandered through the house. It was nearly bare of furniture. I could find no evidence that my father or Merry had ever lived there, not even a photograph. There were two rooms with single beds and small dressers in them, and one of these bedrooms was strewn with a woman's clothes. I tiptoed into another room where my grandmother, balding and feeble, lay in a hospital bed under a pile of old quilts. There was a smell like sour milk. "Grandmother," I said. She lifted her head and yelled out, in a surprisingly strong voice, "Run, run—the Baptists are after you!" I backed away.

In the den, Merry was bustling about in the corner, unplugging a large TV set and hoisting it from a table onto the floor. A slight red-haired woman wearing a black jumpsuit leaned against the wall with her arms folded, watching Merry. Merry was talking to the woman but not looking at her. "I figured you really didn't need this fancy set," Merry said, "and we can really use it, what with Dick's poor vision." She lifted the little TV she'd taken from the trunk and set it on the tabletop. "There. That'll do fine."

"Does it work?" the red-haired woman said.

"Been working for years. Came from a motel liquidation."

The woman snorted. "I guess it's black and white."

"It's good quality," Merry said, patting the small TV like a pet.

A little while later I stood out in the driveway. Merry sat behind the wheel of her Lincoln, her elbow crooked out the window. She'd only stayed long enough to unload my things and swap TVs, and now she was heading back to Ohio. I held on to her door handle. It was getting dark. "I can't do it," I said.

"It'll go smooth as silk." Merry winked her green eye at me. "Read those want ads every day, sugar. Should be anytime. I'll be back before you know it."

I tried to think of something that would slow her down, if not stop her. "What should I tell Dad?"

"I wouldn't tell him anything." She started the car. "Considering your track record. And his."

"What'd he do?" I said, but she didn't seem to hear me. She stepped on the gas, flicking her hand in a wave as she spun out onto the dirt road.

I watched the red dust settling and thought about Iowa—our two-story white house with its porch swing and our sweet-smelling lawn that rolled under my treehouse down to the cornfield. At home, on a summer evening, the air would be full of humidity and comforting sounds—crickets, country music from passing cars, the distant voice of the baseball announcer at City Park. Daisy would be cooking my father's dinner—maybe pork chops and baked potatoes. I couldn't picture what my mother would be doing because she lived with Smitty, in his Victorian house across town. For years, Smitty and my mother had eaten breakfast together every morning at the cafe, and every afternoon she helped him with his business affairs. Finally, after she'd spent all of Christmas Eve and Christmas Day with Smitty, my father said to her in a joking voice, "You like him better than you do us. Why don't you just move in with him?" She called his bluff and did just that. Since Daisy had already taken over at our house, it wasn't that much of a change.

I stood there in the driveway till the sun had dropped behind the mountains. Then I untied the dog and took him inside.

I got into a routine right away. Every morning at breakfast I read the entire newspaper, saving the lost-and-found ads for last. When I'd finished my Grape-Nuts I placed the bowl on the floor, and Captain Crunch Junior stepped up and licked the bowl clean and then some, causing it to roll around the kitchen floor.

"You kids stop that racket," my grandmother screamed from her bedroom.

The red-haired woman, who turned out to be my grandmother's live-in nurse, sat across the table from me, reading *Silent Spring* by Rachel Carson. She was half Mexican, her name was LeeAnn, she was forty-two, and her hair, she told me, was naturally red.

The first morning I was there she'd said, "Aren't you going to get bored? How long are you staying?"

Merry hadn't warned me against telling LeeAnn about our scheme, but I knew I shouldn't. Besides, having a secret made me feel important. Merry had chosen me to help her, and since I was in a position to help, why shouldn't I? "I'm here on a rest cure," I told LeeAnn. "For my mental health."

"Well then," said LeeAnn. "You'll fit right in."

After breakfast I would grab an apple from the fridge and make three peanut butter sandwiches. In the living room, which was totally empty, I tied a rope to Junior's collar and we set out for a walk down the dirt road toward the mountains. Strange-looking houses lined the road—adobe houses with scraggly yards from which dark-skinned people stared at me. Sometimes I pretended Lisa Lazar skipped along beside us, barefoot, in her silly green bathing suit. The air was clear and dry, and the sky was so blue it almost hurt to look at it. We strolled past cactus plants and lizards sunning themselves on white rocks. To the south were rounded hills with ribbons of pink running through them. The mountains loomed straight ahead. We walked and walked until I let myself realize we must be miles from my grandmother's house. Nobody knows me here, I thought, and nobody knows where I am. That thought was a signal that we'd gone far enough for one day. Junior and Lisa and I found shade under a pine tree and split the sandwiches and the apple.

When we got back, worn out and thirsty, we napped till dinnertime—frozen dinners and Purina Dog Chow that Merry had left. In the evenings I watched the little television in the den with LeeAnn, who was always doing something else at the same time, like sewing a hem or balancing her checkbook. At seven she spoonfed my grandmother her applesauce, and at nine she gave her a sponge bath. During commercials we talked about all kinds of things, including the existence of God. Neither of us believed, although we both wanted to. I couldn't bring myself to tell her about Lisa.

One night, while we were watching "Nightmare Theatre" and LeeAnn was knitting a Nordic sweater, she told me she thought Merry was a sleazebag. "She's sold off every antique, everything of value in this house."

"What's wrong with that, if nobody else wants it?" I said, realizing I sounded just like Merry. "Merry looks out for herself," I said. "I kind of admire that."

LeeAnn shook her head, clacking her needles together. "I think it's disgusting. At least wait till the poor thing's dead."

"So why do you work here?"

"I won't be here forever," she said. "Besides, I always liked Mrs. St. John. I grew up down the road."

"Did you know my father?"

"He used to let me ride his pinto pony." She held up the front of her sweater and admired it. "Merry used to make us kids march around in a parade just so she could be the majorette. Your father was always helping people, fixing things."

This didn't sound like my father. Whenever he was home from his job at the newspaper, he spent hours sitting in his chair, staring out the living room window at the cornfield behind our house, tapping his empty pipe on the edge of the coffee table. Daisy would bring him fresh glasses of iced tea and rub his shoulders, and sometimes he remembered to say, "Thanks, honey." Their behavior sickened and infuriated me, but I knew better than to let on.

LeeAnn resumed her knitting. "You seem like such a well-adjusted kid," she said.

"Young adult," I said, and we both laughed.

Later that night, Junior hopped up onto my bed, settled himself on my feet, and fell asleep. I lay awake, wondering what LeeAnn would think if she knew the truth about my family and the horrible thing I'd done. I wondered if she'd think I was crazy. Other people thought I was.

After the incident with Lisa, my father took me to a psychiatrist in Indianola. He wore a hearing aid and kept asking me how I felt. "Fine," I kept saying, feeling sorry for him.

He sighed. "Is there anything bothering you?"

"Well," I said, "I keep wondering where that girl's parents were when she went out into the deep water. Why weren't they watching her?" The psychiatrist wrote something down in his notebook, and I knew I'd disappointed him.

At night, after my father and Daisy were asleep, I would pace around our house, shredding tissues and gasping for air. During the day, while they were at work, I lay on the couch watching soap operas with the sound off. Once my mother dropped by, dressed in her pale-pink suit, my favorite, the one she wore to the Garden Club meetings. She sat down beside me on the couch, trying to appear calm, but her eyes were fixed and tense, like a cat's. "The whole town knows what you did," she said. "Do you realize your father had to publish an article about it? In Smitty's paper?" My father had worked his way up to editor-in-chief, but my mother never let us forget that Smitty owned the paper. She grabbed my ankle and shook it. "Why would you attack the little girl? What were you thinking?"

I couldn't stand seeing my mother, the president of the Magruder Garden Club and Ladies' Literary Society, behaving like this. I couldn't stand her helpless hand-wringing. I said, "I hated that girl's frilly bathing suit."

My mother burst into tears. "What's wrong with you?" she said, but didn't wait for an answer. She got up and ran out of the room.

Junior, a hot weight at the end of the bed, let out a loud snore. I jerked my feet out from under him, but he didn't wake up. I knew what was wrong with me, and my mother did too, even though she pretended otherwise. I had become a delinquent because I did not intend to take my turn as Daddy's nursemaid. I did not intend to make myself useful.

After my first day in New Mexico, I didn't go in to see my grandmother again. It was too depressing. I never called home, and when they called me I said I was having a very educational experience. I told my father that Merry was off on a short business trip—going to some motel liquidations—and that she'd left me in the care of Grandmother's nurse, LeeAnn, and that LeeAnn had taken me sightseeing on her days off. I mentioned some places I'd read about on the back of the New Mexico state map.

"How's Mom?" he asked me.

"Sweet," I said. "But kind of confused." I told Daisy I'd bought a square-dancing dress with the fifty dollars she'd given me and she pretended to be horrified.

Once my mother called and said that she'd seen Lisa's mother in the Jack and Jill, and that Lisa was doing fine. "Outwardly," my mother added. Every night Junior slept at the foot of my bed.

The ad appeared after I'd been in New Mexico nearly a week. "Lost: Yellow Lab, from a convenience store near Española. 2 years old. Goes by Captain Crunch. Reward. Call Steve and Cyndi Richardson."

That morning Junior and I walked past the horse pasture, past the school bus converted into a house. We kept following the road when it turned and climbed uphill through some pine trees. A hawk circled overhead, screeching. We'd never gone this far before. Lisa turned and ran back down the hill. I realized that the real Lisa no longer looked like the girl in the bathing suit. For one thing, the bathing suit wouldn't fit. She was a year older. She was bigger, taller, and smarter.

Junior stopped and gazed back at me, questioning.

"Lisa may not ever want to swim again," I said. "Did you know that?"

He sat down on his haunches, his eyes on my sack of sand-wiches.

The phone number in the ad was busy till eight-thirty that night. "He showed up at my door hungry and weak, like he'd walked a long way," I told Cyndi. "Does your dog have a little white spot on the crown of his head?" Merry had coached me on what to say.

"Yes!" Cyndi shouted. "You're the first person who's mentioned the spot. I've gotten four calls already, and nobody's mentioned the spot. It's him, Steve. We found him!"

"I'll send you a picture, so you'll know for sure." I tipped back in my chair, feeling cocky. Merry had taken a picture of Junior, a tad blurry, and it was already in an envelope with the address and a stamp on it.

"You don't have to," Cyndi said. "I can tell by your voice that Crunch is right there in the room. We'll be there in three days."

"Three days?" I rocked my chair back down with a thud, which startled Junior, who was sprawled out in front of the screen door.

"Give him our love, will you?" Cyndi said. "Tell him we're on our way."

"Would you like to tell him yourself?" But she'd already hung up. "Jesus H. Christ," I said. Junior flopped his tail.

"What was that all about?" LeeAnn stood in the kitchen doorway with her hands on her hips. She wore gym shorts and a T-shirt that said ART WON'T HURT YOU. She said, "What are you and Junior up to now?" She pronounced "Junior" in the Spanish way, *"Hooneor,"* and I loved to hear her say it.

I said, "If you're a real nurse, how come you don't wear a uniform?"

She said, "If you're not a Christian, how come you're talking to Jesus? 'Twilight Zone' is on. Grave robbers. Right up our alley."

"Don't let them leave without him," Merry said on the telephone later that night. "And listen, sugar. About the reward money. Get cash. I'll give you a third."

"I don't want it." Talking to Cyndi, hearing her voice, had made me feel guilty about tricking her.

"I'll start a savings account for you," Merry said. "For college."

"I'm not going to college."

"Escape money, then. In case you get into another jam. You're impulsive, just like Brother."

So this could go on and on, I thought, this getting into one jam after another. "Okay," I said.

"See you on the weekend," Merry said.

"But what if they know I'm lying?"

"Remember. You're not saying he *is* their dog. You're just saying he could be."

I hung up and wandered into the den, where LeeAnn sat in the recliner, finishing up a crossword puzzle, her reading glasses perched on the end of her nose. "Whatever you and Merry are cooking up," she said, "I don't want to know about it."

"It's a losing proposition," I said.

"Six-letter word for 'nuts,'" LeeAnn said.

"Insane." I flopped down on the hairy brown couch. My bare thighs immediately started itching. "What was my father really like?" I said. "Was he some kind of rebel?"

She lowered her newspaper. "Because he held up the liquor store?"

I sank back into the couch, feeling queasy. After a while I said, "How long was he in jail?"

"Not a day," LeeAnn said. "Your grandfather got him and his football buddies off scot-free. They were drunk when they did it, but still. Worst thing that could've happened, him not being held responsible. He slunk off in the dead of night and never came back."

I closed my eyes.

"Didn't you know?" LeeAnn said. "Shoot, I'm sorry. You acted like you did."

"I knew," I said, and I felt like I had. My father had committed a stupid, public act, left his home forever, and was still waiting for his comeuppance. I might be doing the same thing, if Merry hadn't come along. It was much smarter to operate in the gray areas of life, like Merry did. She would never cower, and she'd never wait around for anything. And she'd never get caught.

Cyndi called me at noon from Española on the third day, and I gave her directions to the house. Afterward I sat on the front porch in my white sundress, drinking lemonade and telling myself I was the picture of trustworthiness. LeeAnn had gone to the Laundromat, and when she got back, I was going to tell her that Junior's rightful owners had shown up out of the blue to claim him.

I gazed down the road. With Junior gone, I thought, I'd be too afraid to go on hikes, and Lisa had grown up and left us. That's what I was focusing on then—how bored I'd be without them.

A dusty gray Volvo pulled into the driveway. Cyndi stepped out first, smoothing down her flowered smock. She was very pregnant. "Tabitha?" she said, starting toward me. That was the name I'd given. My alias.

I set down my glass and jumped up to greet her. Confidence, I told myself. Pretend you're Merry.

Steve climbed out of the driver's side. He wore a sweaty T-shirt and running shorts, as if he hadn't even bothered to change from his run before heading off across the country. He looked at me skeptically and didn't speak. I knew then that this trip was Cyndi's idea.

"Hello," I said, shaking Cyndi's damp hand. Her hair was long and wavy, pulled back in a messy ponytail. She had a large, pleasant face. I said, "How was the drive?"

"Horrendous," Steve said. "Illinois. And then Missouri."

"Would you like some lemonade?" I said.

"Where is he?" said Cyndi. "Where's Crunch?"

I'd shut Junior in my bedroom, because I thought they should see him first in a dim light. "Resting," I said. "It's his nap time."

When I opened the bedroom door, my knees were shaking. Junior reclined on my bed like a prince. He raised his head but didn't get up. Cyndi gasped and covered her mouth.

Steve crouched down on the floor. "Crunch. Come here, boy."

Junior stared at them. "He doesn't remember us," Cyndi said, swaying on her feet. "Is that possible?"

"He's not awake yet," I said. "Wake up, Junior." He leapt up and pranced over to sit on my foot. I said, "I've been calling him Junior."

"Junior." Steve patted the floor. Junior went to Steve, wagging his tail. I held my breath. Steve scratched Junior's ears and then inspected him all over, even examining his teeth. Finally Steve looked up at me, but I couldn't read his expression. "Thank you," he said gravely.

Cyndi plopped down on my bed, her face pale. "I still can't believe it. I haven't been able to sleep, my blood pressure's gone up. My due date's six weeks."

"Sit," Steve said to Junior. Junior licked Steve's face. "Lie down," Steve said. Junior jumped up and put his paws on Steve's chest. Steve said, "He doesn't remember anything I taught him."

"Dumb dog," I said.

"Crunch," Cyndi called in a soft voice, and Junior trotted over and hopped up on the bed beside her. "Now he remembers," she murmured, hugging him. "He remembers. Hello, Crunch."

What if it really is Crunch, I thought. It could be. Or Crunch reincarnated. I started to cry, and I imagined Merry shaking her head in disgust.

"Are you sad about giving him up?" Cyndi said. "I'm sorry. I've only been thinking about myself."

"He's not Crunch," I said. "He's Junior. *Hooneor*."

Cyndi frowned at Steve. "Where are your parents?" Steve said.

"My grandmother," I gestured with my head. "She's senile." I wiped my nose on the back of my hand and then wiped my hand on my white sundress.

"I'm sure you're upset," Cyndi said. "You can get another dog."

"No," I said. "I'm trying to tell you. This dog came from the pound."

Cyndi and Steve exchanged concerned looks. "We're just glad you found him," Cyndi said, scooping up Crunch and handing him over to Steve. Crunch lay awkwardly in Steve's arms with his legs sticking straight out, and they both stroked him under the chin. They didn't care whether or not Junior was Crunch. They loved him no matter what.

"I almost drowned someone," I said. "I was scared and I took it out on her."

Cyndi patted my shoulder. "You'll be okay, Tabitha," Steve said.

"My name's not Tabitha, it's Sophie St. John," I said. "My parents sent me out here from Iowa for the summer, but my grandmother doesn't even know me." I stopped crying, and my heart began to pound. I could feel their generosity infecting me. "You're not suckers," I said. "You're good people."

"That's nice," Cyndi said. She turned to Steve. "We should get going."

Crunch began to squirm and Steve dumped him onto the floor. "I hate to leave Sophie here," Steve said to Cyndi. "We could give her a ride back to Iowa. It's on the way."

Cyndi slipped her arm around Steve's waist and sagged against him, but she didn't protest. I sensed they were playing some sort of game, a game in which they took turns leading valiant, ill-conceived rescue missions. One proposed a course of action most people would consider absurd, and the other went along as though it all made perfect sense. Their game, the kindness and futility of it, and the way it bonded them together, made me like them even more.

"Why don't you call your parents?" Steve said. "We've got room in the car."

I sat down on the edge of my bed and blew my nose, remembering the last time I'd been home. Merry and I had swung by Magruder on our way to New Mexico. She stayed in her Lincoln, listening to the radio, while I went inside. My mother was there for the occasion. One by one they came forward and kissed me, blank-faced, like I was in my coffin and they'd already cried themselves out. Daisy slipped me a fifty-dollar bill. "Buy yourself a summer dress," she said. My father hugged me with one arm, his face turned away. "See you soon," my mother said, opening the door like a hostess at a party. They seemed united, more like a family, with me gone.

Steve and Cyndi were watching me, waiting for my decision. "Thanks anyway," I said.

I followed them out onto the front porch, Junior trotting between them like their long-lost son. Cyndi and Junior climbed into the car, but Steve stopped in the driveway. "Is a check okay?"

I had forgotten about the reward money. "Don't worry about it," I said.

"That was the agreement," Steve said, turning toward the car. "I'll get my checkbook."

During the night my grandmother died in her sleep. LeeAnn discovered her in the morning and called the funeral home. After the coroner pronounced her dead, the funeral-home men took her away, wrapped in one of her quilts. LeeAnn and I spent all morning on the phone. We couldn't reach Merry. She was already on the road somewhere between Ohio and New Mexico. My father said they'd come out to New Mexico as soon as they could get a flight.

In the afternoon I asked LeeAnn if she wanted to go for a

walk. The sky was clouding up behind the mountains, but we set out anyway. "We get storms every day in midsummer," LeeAnn said. "No biggie."

"I never got to know Grandmother," I said. "I wish I felt sadder. I'll miss Junior more than I will her."

LeeAnn, striding along beside me in shorts and hiking boots, just nodded. It had never occurred to me that LeeAnn would own a pair of hiking boots. It was odd seeing her outside, in the daylight, moving along with such assurance that she seemed to leave an impression in the air behind her, like an echo. I realized she'd been walking on this road for years. "What are you going to do now?" I asked her. "Where will you go?"

"I've got a husband in Santa Fe," she said. "I need to make amends and move on."

I waited for her to elaborate, but she didn't. "Me too," I said. Some day I would have to talk to Lisa, the real Lisa, face to face. A gust of wind kicked up the dust around us, sending a plastic cup flying past our feet. We bowed our heads and kept walking. Clouds rolled over us and I felt the first drops of rain. LeeAnn stopped and pointed to an adobe house with a rail fence around it. I'd gotten used to seeing it every day on my walks. "That's where I used to live," she said, and we stood there in the rain looking at the house, which was for me transformed into something mysterious. The windows in front were open, and white lace curtains whipped in the wind.

When Merry pulled into the driveway that evening, I left LeeAnn in the kitchen and went out on the front porch to get it over with. Merry nosed her Lincoln right up to the steps like she was docking a boat, then she climbed out, brushing her hair from her eyes with a bejeweled hand. She was wearing the purple caftan, which was stained between her breasts. Coffee, or chocolate. "I'm beat," she said.

I sat down on the top porch step, wishing I didn't have to give her bad news.

She came up and sat on the step beside me. "Run get the money," she said.

I forced myself to look in her eyes, which were both brown. "I've got a check, made out to me. I think we should split it fifty-fifty." I'd practiced saying this in front of the mirror, but even so, my voice lacked authority.

She sighed dramatically and dropped her head. "And I've got a funeral to pay for."

"How did you know about the funeral?"

"I picked up negative vibes all across Missouri," she said, "but I didn't want to believe them. Finally I pulled over and called Brother."

We sat in silence, looking out at the sagebrush. My mouth was so dry I couldn't swallow. Merry glanced at her watch. "Holy moly." She stood up and jumped off the steps. "Help me get my stuff in, sugar," she said, dashing around to the rear of her car. "Then we need to carry some furniture out of the house. A man's coming for it in half an hour." She opened up the trunk and peered at me around the lid. "We have to do it before Brother gets here. He'll try to lay claim to the whole kit and kaboodle." Her face disappeared and I could hear her rummaging around in the trunk.

I remembered what LeeAnn had said about Merry the majorette, making all the kids march behind her in a parade. I could see there would never be a halt unless I called it. "You're on your own, Aunt Merry." I hadn't practiced saying this, but it sounded as if I had.

Just then LeeAnn yelled through the open window, "Fried chicken!"

Merry slammed her trunk shut and blew past me into the house. I went in behind her, walking at a leisurely pace.

The following summer, when I was sixteen, I got a part-time job at the Magruder City Pool. They put me down in the basement of the rec center, next to the locker rooms. I sat on a stool behind a battered wooden counter, collecting admission fees and handing out wire baskets and locker keys attached to large safety pins. Most of my earnings I put in a savings account I'd started with my half of Steve and Cyndi's check. Escape money.

One Saturday afternoon, after a heavy rainfall, when the pool was virtually empty, Lisa and her mother came through. Lisa's hair was cut in a bob and she wore a Speedo bathing suit. Her mother, a beautiful, haggard-looking woman, trailed behind her, wearing thongs with big plastic daisies on them, smoking a cigarette.

"Hello, Lisa," I said. My face flushed and I wished I'd kept my mouth shut.

Lisa looked up. She didn't recognize me or even seem to wonder how I knew her name. "Hi," she said. She grabbed her mother's hand and tugged. "I'm going off the high dive. First thing."

Her mother smiled at me and rolled her eyes. She didn't recognize me either. "We got a show-off here." She slid some change across the counter. "The diving board at the club isn't as high as this one."

I held out their baskets and keys, and Mrs. Lazar took them. I had to say something more to Lisa. "I'm the one who held you underwater. Two summers ago." I smiled idiotically. "Sorry."

Lisa nodded. "Okay." She started running down the hall toward the women's dressing room. "Cowabunga!" she yelled.

There was a line forming behind Mrs. Lazar. She glared at me, gearing herself up to give me a piece of her mind, even though, I could tell, she'd rather not be bothered. She took a drag of her cigarette. "I sincerely hope you got rehabilitated up in Des Moines," she said.

"I did," I said. "Completely."

Kids in line were pushing and shoving. Mrs. Lazar kept glaring at me, waiting for me to grovel. The ash on her cigarette was ready to drop onto my counter.

"But then again," I said, "I might do the same thing anytime. Or worse."

"I see," she said. She turned and addressed a suntanned woman behind her. "I guess they let anyone work here. This place used to have some class."

"Hurry up," barked the suntanned woman.

Mrs. Lazar shook her head in a world-weary way and flip-flopped off down the hall, flicking her ash on the floor as she went.

The suntanned woman handed me a crumpled dollar bill. "Some folks think they run the world," she said. "If you know what I mean."

"I do," I said. "I certainly do."

Doodlebug

O N E   J A N U A R Y evening, the husband steps into his house and sees his wife kneeling in the middle of the kitchen floor. Her eyes are red, and she stares up at him in that vacant way that means she has just stopped crying. She is wearing his purple sweater, one she knitted for him when they were first married, ten years ago. It looks better on her, he thinks. He goes over to her, squats down and tries to hug her, but she ducks under his arm.

"I hate them," she says in an angry burst.

He knows she is talking about their daughters. "You don't mean that." He gets to his feet and stands there, in his heavy overcoat, trying to adjust to being home. The gleaming white surfaces and fluorescent lights, the purple sweater, the sound of her harsh words, the pungent smell of beef stew, are a shock to his senses.

"Look," his wife says, extending her arm. Three tarnished silver beads nestle in her palm. "Look what they did. This is all I have left." She thinks of swallowing the beads, popping them into her mouth one by one.

Her husband sits down in a wooden chair and tugs off his wet rubber boots. "Maybe I can fix it," he says. The beads are from an old necklace he's seen in her jewelry box, one in a tangle of other old necklaces she never wears.

She looks up at him. The sight of his earnest face calms her.

"Or we'll get you a new necklace," he says.

"It's not just that." She closes her fingers tightly over the beads. "At least you get out and see people."

He shrugs off his overcoat. "Believe me, I wish I didn't," he says. He works as an associate dean at a large midwestern university and this is 1968. He had a counseling session that day with a freshman, a Jewish boy from New York who was complaining about the fact that none of his teachers would call him by his chosen name, Little Eagle. He thinks of telling his wife about this, because he knows she would laugh, but she speaks first.

"I'm taking the evening off," she announces. "Can you keep them out of my hair?"

All afternoon he's been thinking of the moment when he will pull back the covers of their bed, slide down, and extinguish himself in sleep. "Let me catch my breath first," he says.

Later, after supper, he ushers his daughters into the living room. Still in his work clothes—white shirt, red paisley tie, and gray wool trousers—he settles down on the couch, shifting on a loose spring. His daughters, Jessie and Magda, wearing their pajamas, sit at his feet, subdued and solemn.

Outside, snow is falling, and the limbs of the oak trees are already white. Wind sings around the corners of their old frame-house. Tomorrow, when Jessie and Magda wake up, there will be a foot of fresh snow on the ground, and school will be canceled. The girls will pester their mother all day about letting them make snow-cream, which she will finally agree to.

His wife has retreated to the bathroom for a hot bath, but her husband feels her presence as if she were sitting there in the dining room, judging him. "What should we play?" he asks, more of himself than his daughters. He hasn't played with them in a long time. Nowadays, since they are both in school, he prefers to help them with homework or read to them.

"What would *you* like to play?" Jessie says. She is feeling benevolent because today, at school, she was named "Scholar of the Week" by the principal. Jessie is seven, the older daughter, serious-looking in her tortoiseshell glasses. Her first words, her parents proudly told her, formed a complete sentence. Jessie's dark hair is waist length, and her mother fixes it every morning in two plaits—fat and luscious at the top, narrowing toward the end in an ugly way that Jessie doesn't like, but says nothing about, because she doesn't want to hurt her mother's feelings.

Her father is in his late thirties, still trim and agile, but tonight he sags back into the couch, feeling like an old man.

Jessie studies her father's tired eyes, the way his shoulders droop. His new haircut is too short and emphasizes his receding hairline.

Her father recognizes a worried look on Jessie's face, and he is reminded of himself as a child, when he worried all the time about everything. He spent most of his childhood in an orphanage. He would lie on his cot at night, in a soggy-smelling cavernous room full of other cots and other boys, and just as he was about to fall asleep a worry would snatch him awake—suppose his father had a wreck on his way to the orphanage for visitors' day? Suppose the floor beneath him suddenly collapsed from the weight of all the beds?

The father gropes among his boyhood memories, searching for a happy one. He leans forward. "How about we play Cowboys and Indians?"

"No thank you," says Magda. She is five—round-faced and pouty, with a blond pixie haircut and an air of self-absorption that her sister envies and her parents fear.

"Come on, pie," the father says to Magda. "Be fun."

Magda shakes her head.

Jessie tries to look interested in his game, but she is disappointed. She and her best friend have recently invented their own game, one which involves staying outside for as long as they can stand it. They tromp through the snow, arm in arm, chanting, "Accustomed to the long, cold, Siberian winters . . ." Jessie glances outside now, at the snow whirling around the bay windows, icing the ground, transforming the familiar woods and ravines around her house into a fairyland. This, she thinks, would be a grand night to play Siberia.

The father sees that his girls will take some convincing. "I used to love Cowboys and Indians," he says. "Doodlebug Clark and I played every day after school. It was our favorite game."

"Doodlebug?" Magda pulls up one leg of her pajama bottoms and pats a scab on her knee. Magda listens carefully to everything, although she appears not to. She frowns at her scraped knee, her tongue peeking out between her lips. She thinks of Doodlebug as a large, scampering ladybug, a giant version of the one she kept as a pet in a matchbox last summer.

"Doodlebug was my pal at the orphanage," the father says. "I can't remember his real name. He only stayed there one summer."

"Why was he called Doodlebug?" Jessie says.

"I've no idea," her father says. He hasn't thought of Doodlebug in years. The harder he tries to remember Doodlebug, the more elusive Doodlebug becomes. He can only catch a glimpse of him from the corner of his mind's eye—a thin child with a crewcut, slightly bulging eyes, a blue and white striped shirt. Much more vivid in his memory is the long, dusty alley he and Doodlebug played in, the heat and intensity of the sun on his face, the scratchy leaves of a holly bush near the back gate of the orphanage. He remembers himself and Doodlebug running, laughing, leaping for joy. Those were the happiest moments of his life, he thinks. It feels very important to him to play Cowboys and Indians now with his daughters.

Jessie smiles back at her father, although his smile makes her nervous. She thinks about last summer, when her father took them to Little Rock, and they drove past the old brick orphanage where he used to live. It had been turned into a nursing home. Jessie saw mostly black faces on the street, so she pictures Doodlebug as a black boy, fierce, shiny, and wild in an Indian costume. Her father, looking like he does today, only smaller, swaggers along in a vest, chaps, and a Stetson hat. Did Doodlebug carry a knife? she wonders. The idea excites her, then frightens her. "Let's play," she says, clasping her hands in front of her. "I'll be the good guy."

Her parents expect Jessie to become a teacher, like her father, and she will. One afternoon, years from now, in a city far from home, she will do a project with her kindergarten students. She will have them dip their feet in paint and make prints on a roll of shelf paper. The students will be delighted, the little Jasons and Andrews and Samanthas and Ashleys, by their own individual marks, life-size and important, autographed underneath. The project will have the opposite effect on Jessie. She will be overwhelmed by the sight of the little blue, yellow, red, and green feet, one pair after another, insignificant and interchangeable. She will have to go into the hall for a minute, to collect herself, to stop herself from wondering what she has done with her life.

Magda squeezes her father's ankle. "If we play Cowboys and Indians I get to be Doodlebug," she says. She's still thinking of her pet ladybug. She only had him one day, but she loved him all the same. She stuffed a raisin in the matchbox for him to eat, and named him "Quelle Heure" after something she heard her mother ask her father, when they were all riding together in the car. Magda thought the words must be magic, because they caused her father, who was driving, to answer in French, and then lean over and kiss her mother on both cheeks.

Her mother laughed with delight. In the backseat, Jessie and Magda hugged their dolls.

When Magda was training Quelle Heure to sit on the tip of her finger, he flew away. She chased him across the yard and watched him disappear into the summer dusk. For a long time she stood there, in the middle of the lawn, at the spot where he'd vanished, holding out her finger, in case he wanted to come back.

"Daddy," she says now. "Let me be the Doodlebuggy." She cuts her eyes at him in a way she knows is charming.

He winks at her.

Despite what her parents think, Magda will not grow up to be a flirt, because she is not able to withhold, or be deceptive. She becomes a woman who flushes easily, a woman who stamps her foot at the world's unfairness. A natural mother, she will never have children. When she is forty years old, she will sit in this same room, on the couch, and read British mystery novels, waiting for her younger lover to call her on the telephone. It will be impossible for her to leave her parents and this house, with its high ceilings and tall windows and walls covered with oil paintings, this house which even on a bright summer day will feel to Magda like it does now—a spot of cozy lamplight in the darkness.

Magda turns to Jessie. "I'm buggy, see?" She flops on her back, kicks her arms and legs in the air like a bug.

Jessie is irritated by her sister's silliness. "I'll be you, Daddy," Jessie says. "Were you the cowboy? Were you the good one?"

"Cowboys can be good or bad," says her father, updating his game for the sixties.

He hears his wife moving about in the next room—the thud of logs as she drops them into the fireplace.

"Nobody's good all the time," his wife calls.

"I am," Magda says.

"You're bad all the time," Jessie says, swatting at her.

The father is annoyed by his wife's intrusion. He grips

Jessie's knee and then Magda's. "You can take turns being the Cowboy and the Indian. That's what Doodlebug and I did." He is pleased at remembering this tidbit about himself and Doodlebug, the mysterious boy who was once his best friend.

Jessie bounces up and down. "Will you be on my side?"

"He's on mine," Magda says, and sits up, serious again.

The father looks at his daughters, at both of them wanting him. Suddenly he feels twenty years younger. He gets down onto the floor on his hands and knees. His red tie hangs down, touching the carpet. "I'm a horse," he says. "Doodlebug and I never had a horse. Y'all are lucky. You can take turns riding me." He shakes his head like a horse, and he sees a silver bead, one from his wife's necklace, glinting under the couch. He decides not to say anything about it then, because he doesn't want to interrupt their game.

"My turn!" Magda jumps up and clambers onto her father's back.

He paws the ground and whinnies. "Breeeeee."

You must be kidding, Jessie thinks, but she says nothing. She is disturbed by the sight of her adored father, so willing to go down on his hands and knees. She hopes her mother will come in and put a stop to this nonsense.

The father flicks his tie over his shoulder. "Grab my reins," he says.

Magda pulls the tie from side to side. She spurs her father's ribs with her slippered feet and shouts, "Giddy up, go on."

"Dear Miss Jess," her father says, aware of her discomfort. "You can be the cowboy. Let Magda set up camp in the kitchen and then you come after us."

"I don't want to," she says. "It's a stupid game. What's so great about it?"

"You're being ugly, Jess," Magda says, imitating their mother.

Their father pouts in an exaggerated way, feeling like he couldn't stop himself from acting silly if he had to. "Come on, kiddo, don't disappoint me." He crawls over, with Magda hanging onto his neck, and nuzzles Jessie's chest. "Don't disappoint Mr. Horse."

Jessie jumps up.

"Is you my pardner or isn't you?" he says.

"Yes. I am." She folds her arms on her chest.

"All right then," he says. "We're off, Pocahontas."

Magda makes a whooping sound and rides her father into the kitchen.

Jessie stands still, staring at the carpet, not knowing what to do. Her father scares her. His nuzzle seems like a shameful plea. He has just shown her a flash of his need for her, a need they will both become more aware of as the years go by. Even now, it feels like a burden. She wonders if her mother can relieve her of it. She turns, walks toward the living room, and peers around the corner.

Her mother, fresh from the bath, her smooth hair brushed out around her shoulders, sits in a rocking chair in front of the fireplace, soaking up the warmth of the fire she's just made. The room smells of cedar.

Jessie wants to go sit in her mother's lap, but something stops her in the doorway. "Mama," she says, even though her mother prefers to be called "Mother."

"What, honey."

"Do I have to play with them?"

The mother closes her eyes, and tilts her head back. Her daughters are lucky, she thinks, having a father who wants to spend time with them. "You don't have to," she says finally. "But it would be nice if you wanted to."

She looks up, but Jessie is no longer there. The mother suspects that, once again, she's said the wrong thing. She hears Jessie walking, heavy-footed, toward the kitchen.

The fire crackles, shooting a spark out onto the brick hearth, but she can't bring herself to put up the screen just yet. She's wrapped herself in an afghan and still she's cold. She is sick and tired of winter, of living up north, on the "planet zero," as she calls it. She misses her hometown of Dumas, Arkansas.

While rocking in her chair, the mother has been trying to write a letter, but she can't concentrate on it. She is listening to her husband and children in the next room, and she feels like a stranger in her own house. She has never heard her husband mention Doodlebug, and wonders if he's invented him to entertain the girls. Better that than something he's never shared with her. She knows her jealousy is absurd, but this is the way she feels. All of her emotions are boiling together in a small pot.

She has been thinking of her sixteenth birthday, a warm day in late May. She sees her parents' house in Dumas—a white stucco house with a red tile roof. She is sunbathing in the backyard, wearing plaid shorts and a sleeveless blouse, lying on her stomach on an old quilt, reading a fashion magazine, one knee bent in what she imagines is a sophisticated pose. Suddenly her own Daddy, just back from a long business trip, comes out of the house and into the backyard. The screen door slaps closed behind him. He is wearing his usual felt hat and chomping on an unlit pipe. He walks over and gives her a necklace. A beautiful silver necklace from Mexico, like nothing he's given her before, or will ever give her again. He doesn't wrap it up, and he doesn't present it to her ceremoniously. He drapes it from her dangling bare foot and says, "Merry Christmas, glamour-puss."

Now, at the fireplace, the mother looks down at the letter in her lap, the one she's been writing to her own mother. In it she is saying the things she wanted to say to her husband. She has written: "Today I lost the last physical link I had with Daddy. One of the girls (probably Magda, she's had her eye on it) took the necklace Daddy gave me, the one with the hollow silver beads, out of my jewelry box. I think the two of them must've started fighting over it. Anyway, they broke the chain and the beads scattered. When they were collecting the beads, they stepped on and crushed most of them. I know they didn't do it on purpose, but I was so angry I couldn't see straight. I wanted to kill them."

She reads her words over, through her mother's eyes. These words will upset her mother, who now lives alone, and to whom family harmony means everything. Her mother, a Southern lady, has a platitude for every occasion.

She imagines her mother's reply. "Don't be so hard on yourself," her mother will write back. And then, in her delicate, barely legible handwriting, "Remember, love is not a feeling. Love is an action."

The mother sighs and scoots her chair closer to the fireplace. She has heard these platitudes all her life. What she hates most about them are the splinters of truth they contain.

She crumples up the letter, tosses it into the fire, and watches as the edges start to glow. The entire ball of paper burns red and quivers, then turns black. Just two more hours, the mother thinks, and we'll all be asleep in our beds. Two more hours, and this day will be over.

The First Paper Girl in
Red Oak, Iowa

S N O W   B L E W in sheets across the pavement so that Cherry couldn't tell where the interstate ended and the cornfield began. Gusts of wind nudged the sides of her station wagon, and snow swirled across the windshield like a deliberate smokescreen. A green exit sign loomed up in the whirling snow, and without letting off the gas, she turned the car uphill toward what she hoped was the exit ramp. The needle on the gas gauge read E. Cherry's leg shook so that her knee bumped the steering wheel. "Cokes all around," she said to her children in the backseat. "Okay?"

"No thanks," Mo said.

Linc's head appeared over the seat. His sweatshirt hood was pulled up and tied under his chin. With his wire-rimmed glasses and scandalized expression, he was an eight-year-old version of his father. "Mom, I've been thinking," he said. "If the heater stops, we might get frostbite. They'll have to cut our feet off."

"Then we'll get some nice new artificial feet." Cherry managed to get the car up the ramp and, tapping the brakes, inch down into an Amoco station. She was sure that if she drove anywhere near the gas island, the car would slide into the pumps and cause a huge explosion. She imagined the three of them flying through the air with surprised expressions on their faces and had to squeeze her lips together to keep from laughing. She knew she was on the verge of hysteria.

She eased to a stop next to the gas station office and left the car running. The windows were steamed up, but she could see two men behind the counter. "Sit tight," she said.

"I'm coming in," Mo said, already opening her door. "You said Cokes."

"I thought you didn't want one."

"When I say no, I mean yes," Mo said. "And when I say yes, I mean no."

Linc said, "Alan Shepard had to pee in his space suit." He was reading a book called *Man in Space*.

Inside the office, the air was warm and stuffy. An electric heater squatted on the concrete floor, glaring a frightening shade of orange. A middle-aged man with mutton-chop sideburns sat on a stool, and beside him, perched on a metal folding chair, was a young man with a long neck that seemed to bend in the middle, tilting his chin up. The young man, who had curly, reddish-brown hair, wore a miniature Bible on a chain around his neck. He reminded Cherry of her neighbor back in Logansport, a kind young man who shoveled her driveway when her husband Rainey was out of town.

"What brings you out in this weather?" the older man asked. "State Patrol is telling everyone to stay off the roads."

Cherry's stomach lurched. The anxiety she'd managed to contain by focusing on driving suddenly seized her. She didn't know how she was going to make herself get back on the highway. She forced a smile. "Fill it up, please." She handed her car keys to the older man. "Where am I?"

"Shelbyville, Indiana, USA," he said, sliding off the stool.

"We knew the last two," said Mo. "Is there a motel around here? With an indoor pool?"

"Right up the road," said the older man, and disappeared out into the snow.

Cherry turned her gaze on the young man, who blinked nervously. "Hi," he said, fingering the little black Bible on his chain.

Cherry nodded at him, aware of his eyes on her. She'd left her coat in the car, and she was still wearing her church clothes—a slim-fitting wool dress and pumps. She'd been sitting in church listening to another one of Pastor John's dull sermons when she'd been struck by inspiration. It hadn't been snowing when she piled the kids and luggage into the car and started out. Now she could see how rash she'd been, but she didn't want to give up. This trip felt like the only adventurous thing she'd done in years. She looked at the young man. "What are your plans for the next few days?" she asked him.

He frowned. "Excuse me?"

"I'll pay you two hundred dollars to ride with us to Virginia Beach, Virginia."

The young man slipped a worn leather glove on his hand and flexed his fingers in it. "You don't mean it," he said. "I work here, anyway."

"What do you want him for?" Mo said. She moved next to Cherry and pressed a cold Coke can against Cherry's arm.

Cherry drew her arm away. "I need company. Someone to keep me awake at three in the morning."

Mo tossed her ponytail. "I can do that," she said. "We'll sing camp songs."

"I need a man along," Cherry said.

The toilet flushed in the next room.

"You've got Linc," Mo said.

"I have to get there quick, you see," Cherry said to the young man.

He looked down at his glove.

"Two-fifty," Cherry said. "Final offer." She had four hundred dollars in her purse—the maximum amount the automatic teller would give her.

"Why don't you use that money and stay here till the weather clears?" he said. "I don't want to ride to Virginia Beach. Don't even know where it is."

"It's in Virginia," Mo said. "And it's on the beach. There'll be palm trees and we can go swimming. Mom bought me a new two-piece. I've got it on under here." She plucked at her pink crewneck sweater.

"It won't be that hot in Virginia," said the young man, cocking his head even farther back.

Cherry felt a wave of irritation at the way he sat there as though they had all the time in the world. "It might very well be that warm, on the coast," she said, smiling at Mo, who was frowning suspiciously at her.

"There'd have to be a tropical heat wave," the young man mumbled. He swiveled around and peered out the window at Cherry's car, giving it the once-over, the same way he'd given her the once-over. "I do have vacation time coming," he said.

"Run ask your boss," she said. "Two hundred and fifty dollars. Half now, half later."

"It's not the money." He pulled off the glove and slapped his leg with it. "I'll go," he said, as though it had been his idea all along.

The older man blew back through the door, his sideburns white with frost. "You owe me," he said to the young man. "I'm a dadburn block of ice."

The young man popped up off the stool. "Tiny, I'm going to drive these folks to Virginia Beach for two hundred and fifty bucks!"

———

While the young man went home to explain to his parents and pack, Cherry and the children ate at Howard Johnson's. It was past eight o'clock when they started out again, with the young man driving. His name was Nick. Nick of Time, Cherry called him.

Linc, who'd had two Tommy Tucker Turkey Dinners, fell asleep in the backseat. Mo read a Laura Ingalls Wilder book with a flashlight she kept in her travel kit.

Cherry tried to have a conversation with Nick. "I'm from Iowa," she said. "Ever been there?"

"Never been west of the Mississippi," he said, almost proudly, Cherry thought. His hands were in the ten and two o'clock positions on the wheel.

In their headlights the snow twirled in circles like Mo's kaleidoscope. Pretty, Cherry thought, if you aren't the one driving. "Do you like to travel?" she asked Nick.

Nick shrugged. "Not particularly." The car was warm, but he was still wearing his green army jacket with a denim jacket underneath. On his head was a plaid deer-hunting cap with the flaps tied up.

"How old are you?" she asked him.

He smiled, still looking straight ahead. "Nineteen. How old are you?"

"How old do I look?"

"I can't remember what you look like."

Mo lurched forward and shone her flashlight in Cherry's face. "Now how old is she?" Mo said.

Cherry tucked her hair behind her ear.

"Twenty-nine."

"Close," Cherry said, pushing Mo's flashlight away. She wondered if he was joking, or if he really thought she looked twenty-nine. Either way, the trip was going much faster with him along.

————

"Welcome to Kentucky!" Mo shouted. They were crossing a bridge over the Ohio River. The snow had turned to rain and was coming down in bursts, like handfuls of pea gravel.

Linc started awake. "Are we on the right road?" he said.

"We're hopelessly lost," Cherry answered.

"Hand me the map," said Linc.

"We'll be there before you know it," Cherry said to him. And then, enjoying the larger audience, she went on. "I used to have so much fun at the beach when I was a little girl. Mother and Daddy took me and Tommy to Miami every spring. I just can't wait to get to Virginia Beach."

Nick said, "I've never heard of anyone going to Virginia Beach. It can't be that great."

Cherry wished Nick would keep his opinions to himself.

"Are we really lost?" Linc said.

"How about everyone going to sleep?" Nick said, glancing at Cherry.

"How about keeping your eyes on the road?" Cherry said.

"Road?" Nick said. "What road?"

Mo gave a whoop of laughter and Linc said, "Why's that funny?"

Cherry said, "Got me." She felt as though she and Nick were having a tug-of-war. He kept giving little jerks on the rope, while she was just trying to hold her own. It was a familiar sensation, one she'd felt with the other clerks at Sassy, the clothing store where she worked, with Rainey, even with her own children. And now Nick. She never knew why a tug-of-war started, or what it was about, but tonight it felt not only mental but physical, as if the very next tug would pull her dress right off. She wrapped her arms around herself.

Nick drove them on through Kentucky and into West Virginia. Drifts gave way to dirty strips of snow along the fence rows. Snow like that looked nasty, Cherry thought, like the elastic of someone's underwear showing. If there had to be snow, she'd rather have the ground completely covered.

The rain stopped, the clouds began to break up, and

clumps of stars appeared in the sky. Both children fell asleep, leaning against the doors on opposite sides. Cherry had tried to go to sleep, tucking her stocking feet up under her and leaning against her own door, but she wasn't sleepy. She kept thinking about Rainey, and how he'd ruined their Christmas holidays. The kids were out of school, and Cherry had taken a week off work, but that didn't make any difference to him. Two days after Christmas he'd informed her that he had to leave town, and the next day he'd flown off to a farm-implements-dealer convention in Virginia Beach. She kept imagining Rainey's face when he saw them. She pictured him catching sight of them in the hotel lobby. His confident, composed expression would vanish and he would gape in astonishment. Then, for the children's sake, he would act happy to see her. He wouldn't have the heart to send them home. And after a while, Cherry hoped, he'd be genuinely glad they'd come. This trip—a fourteen-hour drive at night in a blizzard—should prove to him how much they needed him.

Cherry looked over at Nick, who sat in the same slightly stooped position, both hands on the wheel, looking calm and relaxed, as though this were an everyday occurrence. "Penny for your thoughts, Mr. Nickel," she said.

"Oh," he said, and shifted slightly. "I was just thinking about what I might do when I get to Virginia. I might just travel on down the coast."

"Ever been to Florida?"

"Never been south of Mammoth Cave."

"So this is a new experience," Cherry said. "How nice! I'm offering you a real opportunity here." She smiled, reminding herself that she was in charge of this excursion.

"Yeah, well," he said. "Would've done it sooner or later. I was waiting till I got married. So I could travel with my wife. Whoever she ends up being."

"When are you going to get married?"

"When are you going to get divorced?" He grinned, and then he said, "Sorry."

"You should be."

Nick fingered his Bible.

"Apology accepted," Cherry said, but she still felt uneasy. Nick had gotten inside her life too fast. She wasn't sure if he'd just ducked in, or if she'd opened the door too wide. And he'd said the wrong thing. Lately, no matter how hard she tried not to hear it, a voice in her head kept whispering the word "divorce."

Everyone else seemed to be thinking about it too. In the last few months, Mo had begun to play Divorce with her dolls. Every time Cherry heard her she wanted to go in and interrupt, to explain that there was no question of her and Rainey separating. But she knew from the other women at Sassy that all the children were starting to play Divorce instead of Marriage. If anyone had told her, when she was a child, that her dolls should get divorced, she wouldn't have known what they meant.

From what Cherry remembered of her childhood, there had been nobody in the whole town of Red Oak who was divorced. Families were happy and little girls were taken care of. Her father had been the mayor, and he was a member of nearly every local organization, but he made it home for dinner every night. Her mother played the organ at First Methodist Church on Sunday mornings, and she got special permission from Reverend Corkren for Cherry to sit up in the balcony beside her. When her parents weren't looking out for her, her older brother, Thomas, was. He pulled her to school on his sled till she was old enough to cross the streets by herself. When some of the other girls teased her on the playground because she'd won the spelling bee for the third week in a row, Thomas had come to her rescue. He simply leaned against a nearby tree and intimidated them.

Beside her, Nick muttered, "Heard the name Peaches, but never Cherry."

Cherry couldn't tell if he was talking to her, or to himself, so she didn't say anything. But she was gratified that he'd said her name.

For a long time, it seemed, their station wagon was the only car on the interstate. Then, in the westbound lane, a car came toward them with one headlight out and the other shining up at an angle. "If we were in Indiana," Nick said, "a trooper would've pulled that clown over by now." He cleared his throat and added, in a self-important voice, "I installed three seal-beams myself last week."

Cherry considered informing Nick that she, too, was a working person. She could tell him about her job at Sassy, and explain to him that the favorite daytime color this year was breen, a mixture of brown and green—nothing like olive. Or she could tell him that her sports-clothes display had won an award for best in the district. But she didn't think he'd be impressed. Instead she said, "In Red Oak, I used to deliver newspapers in blizzards. Minus thirty and dark as night. Never thought a thing of it. I walked over the top of twelve-foot snowdrifts and dropped papers down on people's porches."

"No kidding."

"I delivered it every other day for four months. The *Red Oak Conservative*."

Nick yawned. "When was this?" he said.

Cherry crossed her legs. She had to use the toilet, but she decided to wait as long as she could. "I was ten. Mo's age. No other girl had delivered papers in Red Oak, but I talked the editor into letting me do it. Mom made me wear a dress and my knees nearly froze off, but I wanted to buy myself a bicycle—a blue Schwinn with a basket and a bell." Cherry had never told this story to anyone before; she was surprised how much she remembered. "When it was below zero," she went on, "the snow was so hard I couldn't scoop it up. My rubber boots squeaked."

"Did you get one?" Nick said.

"One what?"

"A bike."

"Nope," Cherry said. "I never saved a cent, but some of the experiences I had! When I got up, at five o'clock, I was the only living thing on our street. Once, this was summer, I went out and saw the teenage girl next door sleeping on her front lawn. Passed out drunk. I went over and kicked her, not hard, just to wake her up. Another time I saw a strange man crouched up in a little tree. The police came and took him away. Are you interested in all this?"

They passed an old pickup truck with a decorated Christmas tree in the bed.

"Are you interested?"

"Sure," Nick said, and sighed.

"Once I saw a naked woman, kissing a fully clothed man."

Nick snorted. "You looked in people's windows?"

"No. Not exactly." Why had she said that? What she'd actually seen was Reverend Corkren, standing over a heating vent, naked except for his undershirt, which was billowing out around him like a babydoll dress. Cherry thought about describing this scene to Nick. Instead she asked him, "Where'd you get that little Bible?"

"Graduation present from my mother."

"Sweet," Cherry said, but she wondered what his mother had meant by such a gift.

Outside, the fields rolled away toward woods on both sides of the road.

"Iowa's pretty flat, isn't it?" Nick said.

"It's much hillier than Indiana." Cherry felt like she was back on equal footing with Nick. "I quit delivering papers because my mother didn't like it," she told him. "She thought lugging that paper bag around wasn't ladylike."

"My mom didn't like me doing this," Nick said.

"But you're doing it anyway." Cherry was annoyed he had changed the subject. "I didn't want to quit my route, so Mom got Tommy to sneak behind me and pick up the papers I'd just delivered. I didn't know who was stealing them till Mrs. Tully caught him red-handed."

"My mom would like to chain me in the backyard the rest of my life." Nick made a growling sound. "Dad might toss me a bone now and then."

Cherry stiffened. "I'm sure they love you. Just like my parents loved me." She softened her voice. "Maybe mine just knew how to show it better than yours."

"Do you show your kids you love them?"

"Of course." Cherry turned around. If the car doors were to pop open, which one would she try to catch first? She could never decide, because she loved them both the same.

"Your parents weren't perfect," Nick said sullenly.

"I didn't say that." *But they were, they were*, protested a little voice in her head, the same voice that told her that she and Rainey belonged together. Cherry felt a bag of gloom slipping over her.

"I'm going to pull over," Nick said. With one hand he unbuttoned his jacket, lifted off his Bible necklace, and coiled it carefully on the dashboard. "Can you drive awhile?"

"Of course," Cherry said, but she didn't want to. She longed to curl up in bed, fully dressed, like she had when she came back from delivering papers, and sleep till her mother woke her for bacon and fried egg with burnt, lacy edges.

At 1 A.M. Cherry was driving through the mountains of West Virginia. The road rolled boldly up and down long, steep hills. Nick was slouched in the corner, snoring, using his hunting cap for a pillow. Neither Mo nor Linc had made a sound for a long time. Cherry let the car speed up to eighty when they went downhill.

She felt disconnected from the onward-rushing car, from Nick and the children, from herself. The headlights made a tunnel of light in front of her, giving her the sensation that she was burrowing underground. She couldn't breathe.

"Nicholas," she said, pronouncing it "Nickel-ass" and shaking his knee. "Wake up. Keep me company."

He stirred and made a mumbling noise.

She shook his knee again.

"What makes you think," he said in a low, calm voice, "that you can twist my knee? It's not a doorknob."

Cherry thought she must be imagining him saying this, but she removed her hand. Why did she always get stuck with stiffs? She wished she had asked Tiny with his mutton chops to come along, instead of Nick and his Bible. After a few seconds, Cherry told Nick, "By the way, you'll have to go to my husband's hotel to get the rest of your money. I forgot to mention that."

Nick didn't respond.

By the time they crossed over the line into Virginia, Cherry was jumpy and nervous, and resentful that she had to cope with these feelings alone. She swerved when she thought she saw a small man somersault out across the highway. She flinched when she thought she saw red wolf eyes glaring at her from the shoulder of the road. Then, up ahead, she did see something, a shiny object directly in their path. She felt as though they were being drawn toward it. She saw it coming closer, and decided not to swerve around it.

It crunched, and then she heard a loud thump. The rear of the car dropped and pulled to the right, and the tire made a *whomp, whomp, whomp* sound.

"Ease off the gas," Nick said. "Don't touch your brakes. Get over on the shoulder."

Cherry followed his instructions. She was not afraid. She did not feel like any of this was happening to her. I've had a blowout, she thought. The rear of the car dragged like an animal that had been shot. She steered over onto gravel, slowing to a stop. She turned off the ignition and covered her face with her hands.

"What happened?" said Linc. "Are we in Virginia Beach?"

"What'd you hit?" Nick asked Cherry.

She shook her head.

"Oh, maybe it was an animal," Mo said, and began to cry.

"I'll see," Nick said, and jumped out of the car.

Mo said, "I want to go home. Let's turn around and go home."

"We've come too far, honey," Cherry said, but she longed to be back in Indiana too.

Linc said, "Don't forget, Mo. We're going to swim in the ocean."

Mo sniffled.

"Maybe Dad will take us sailing," Linc said.

With part of her mind, Cherry noticed that Linc was rising to the occasion. Like his father would have.

Nick banged on Cherry's window. He was holding on to a twisted hunk of metal as long as his arm.

She rolled down the window.

"Part of someone's fender," he said. "Sliced up your right rear pretty good. You got a spare?"

"Yes." Cherry had no idea whether she did or not.

Nick looked back at the road, which stretched behind them without a curve. "Didn't you see this coming?"

"I'm sorry. I'm so sorry." Cherry wished she could cry, but her eyes remained dry.

Nick kept looking at her. "I don't know about you," he said, "but I want to live."

"I want to live too," Cherry said. How, she wondered, had she ever gotten to the point of having to say such a thing to someone she barely knew?

"Act like it," said Nick.

They stared into each other's eyes. Nick's were round and dark and didn't blink. Cold, damp air filled the car.

Cherry couldn't think how to placate him. "I'm doing my best," she said.

"I am too," said Mo.

Linc said, "All of us are."

Nick rolled up the sleeves of his denim shirt. He said, "Everybody out while I change the tire."

Cherry felt weak with relief. "Thank you," she said. This was the very reason she'd wanted a man along.

"Let's hurry up," said Nick, but he spoke in a friendly way. "It's cold as shit out here," he added absentmindedly, as though, Cherry thought, he'd forgotten who he was talking to.

The children, suddenly bouncing with energy, hopped out of the car and began tussling in the dead grass.

When Cherry stood up her legs quivered, and she knew that if she didn't keep them moving they would collapse under her. She walked back to the tailgate and unlocked it. She scooted a suitcase and Mo's books to the side so she could get at the place where the spare was supposed to be. And sure enough, there it was, snug in its little trough. What if there hadn't been one? Nick might have gone off and left them alone.

Just then, Nick stepped behind the raised tailgate.

She was so glad to see him she said, "You're a dear."

They both leaned into the car to lift the tire out, and Nick's shoulder brushed hers. She turned toward him. He moved closer and they kissed, and then they kissed again. Nick's mouth felt like a small, eager animal. A spot of light flickered through the car window, playing on their faces. Mo's flashlight. Cherry stood up. She couldn't believe what had just happened. "There's the tire," she said loudly, backing away.

While Nick jacked the car up and the children watched him, she walked along the grassy shoulder, her heels sinking into the soft ground. The wind was raw in her face. She was still shaking, but she didn't know if it was due to the blowout or the kiss. Was it an accident? No, because they'd kissed twice. Mo had seen them. Had Linc seen too? She couldn't face Rainey now. But it served him right.

She ran back to the station wagon. "Let's not stop at Virginia Beach," she called out. "Let's keep going to Florida. I'm sure they'll have palm trees."

She stood behind Nick, who was wrestling with the lug nuts. "I'm game," he said, handing her a lug nut to hold. "Long as you're paying."

"Oh you," she said. Nick's sense of humor was only one of the things she loved about him. "Well, what do you think?" she asked the kids. "Walt Disney World?"

They acted like they hadn't heard her. Mo shone her flashlight on the tire, and every now and then turned it on Nick, as though she were studying him. Linc stood beside the highway, waving his arms to slow down cars, even though none were in sight.

Famous POets

IT ALWAYS began the same way. Mother would be sitting at the kitchen table, waiting for supper to cook and reading poetry, usually Edwin Arlington Robinson, or Robert Frost, "somebody who had the decency to rhyme." Sometimes she'd recite these poems to herself, in a stern, matter-of-fact voice, the same voice she'd use to read a newspaper article about an earthquake or a kidnapping.

Father would burst into the kitchen and drop his football-colored briefcase onto the kitchen table. He was a tall man, nearly six-five, with a round, cheerful paunch. "Well, Mr. or Miss So-and-So has agreed to come," he would say. "For an outrageous sum of money, I might add."

Mother would gently shut her book and drum her fingers on the table. "My stars," she'd say, and smile, really just tighten her lips, which was the closest she ever came to smiling.

Dancing through the kitchen on my way here or there, I'd yell, "Who?" and Father would mention some poems Mr. or Miss So-and-So had written, books they'd published, awards they'd won. These things meant nothing to me. I was waiting for him to finish so I could say, "Big deal. Who cares?" I was always trying to see how much I could get away with.

Mother would say, "Watch yourself, Jane," and Father would run his fingers through his thick red hair, a gesture that meant he was eternally put-upon.

Father is an English professor at the university, and back then he was in charge of the "visiting writers" who came to spend a semester "in residence" at the school's expense. Father'd had a few poems published himself, in small literary journals—narrative poems, about his experiences in the war. So he always invited poets, hoping, perhaps, that the next one who came would take an interest in his work. Once they got here, Father was responsible for them, and they always needed lots of looking after. They never seemed to have any attachments, either to family or things. "Like orphans," Father'd say proudly. He'd find them a place to stay, include them in family dinners and outings, cart them around to the grocery store, the doctor, the liquor store. Most of them hadn't written anything in years, didn't write anything here, and didn't write anything after they left here. But they were always well enough known to draw a crowd at readings.

The youngest poet was Mr. R. He spent most of his visit in a campus bar, swilling pitchers of beer with fraternity boys. I first saw him on the cover of his *Selected Poems*, where he was perched on a stool, gazing soulfully into the camera, his hands splayed out on muscular thighs. I was in love with him, until I met him. Then I discovered that his hair was dyed black, his teeth were gray, and he walked funny—holding his shoulders and upper torso stiff while swiveling his hips madly. Also, he said weird things. One time, when he was alone with me, he leaned down and whispered, "Let's you and I go find a train and throw ourselves in front of it." Another time, he told me that his wife back in Texas, a Filipino nurse, was a better wife than any American woman could ever be. I made a gagging gesture behind his back—but deep down I felt insulted. I knew I'd never be a good wife.

Then came Mrs. D, a southern matron who drank sherry on ice and wore a straw hat. She hated the Midwest and refused to fly in or out of Chicago, convinced the Mafia was lurking around every corner. She also refused to stay in the same room with me. Children upset her. So did animals. Once when I was waiting in her backyard for Mother and Father to come out of her apartment, a black cat slunk up and began scratching and yowling at her screen door. Mrs. D appeared, flung open the door, and kicked out at the cat with her sensible shoe, screaming "You don't live here!" She was my parents' favorite, but I hated her guts. I'd prance around the house, wearing my straw cowboy hat, pointing at Mother and Father and chanting "You don't live here, you don't live here" until they sent me to my room.

But the worst one ever was Miss X. She came spring semester, when I was in the ninth grade. She was third choice that year. Father didn't think much of her poetry. "Too sweet," he said. "All ships and clouds." He went on, his face taking on its teacher's smirk, "It's rather like a vine that creeps down and curls around you and, before you know it, chokes the life out of you."

Miss X was in her late seventies, the oldest poet yet. When Father came home from picking her up at the airport he poured himself a glass of bourbon, even though it wasn't noon. "She was in a wheelchair," he said. "I'd no idea she was that far gone." He drained the glass in one swallow. "And you'll never believe what she said to me in the car. She said, 'I've been wanting to kill someone for a long time, and I don't care who it is.' And then she gave me this *look*, you should have seen it."

"Uh-oh," Mother said.

After Miss X met Mother at a party, she began calling Mother day and night, explaining in great detail how someone had done her wrong. Mother would set the phone down on the kitchen counter and pick up her book, and you could hear Miss X cawing through the receiver.

Father told us stories about her temper. "One time, during a party at Princeton, she stomped on her husband's foot and broke his big toe. Her husband retaliated by breaking her arm. Twisted it behind her, till it snapped."

"One can certainly see why," Mother said.

"That's disgusting," I said. "Then what?"

Since it was Mother's job to extend dinner invitations, she managed to keep Miss X at bay until the end of April. But one Saturday morning, when we were sitting around the breakfast table, Father told us he'd taken it upon himself to invite Miss X for dinner that very night. He said, "Ladies, I expect you to be on your best behavior."

Mother stood up without a word, collected her cereal bowl and coffee mug, bore them over to the kitchen sink, and flicked on the hot water full blast. She reached up and began leafing through her copy of *One Hundred and One Famous Poems*, which she kept on the window ledge above the sink, propped open with a smooth black rock from the yard. Through her cotton shirt I could see her bra strap digging into her back.

I reached for more cinnamon toast. The mean streak in Miss X fascinated me. I couldn't wait to meet her, but I knew better than to let on. "God," I said with my mouth full. "That hag?"

Father tilted back in his chair and folded his hands behind his head. He had on the University of Chicago sweatshirt, sleeves shrunk up to his forearms, that he wore on the mornings he shoveled sheep shit. The sheep had been a 4-H project of mine, but when I discovered boys, I'd turned them over to

Father. "She's coming," he said, "whether it suits you or not. Let's try to act civil for a change."

I belched.

That evening, when it was time to pick up Miss X, Father banged out the back door and headed for the driveway, and I followed him. I'd been inside all day, whispering and breathing heavy with my boyfriend on the phone, so walking outside was like stepping into a dream. Father's seersucker suit glowed in the fading yellow light. Behind our house, the sheep were scattered on the hillside, grazing. Our yard was greening up, a bright green, apple green. In the woods across the road, redbud was scattered like pink confetti among the dark tree trunks.

I slipped into the front seat of the station wagon beside Father, and he raised his eyebrows, surprised that I would want to come, but said nothing. In companionable silence, we rattled down the gravel road toward town. It was a cool evening, but I was wearing a heavy cotton sweater, so I rolled down my window to enjoy the smell of wild onions and the sound of red-wing blackbirds on the telephone wires, their calls like screen doors squeaking open. We zipped past my boyfriend's house at the bottom of the hill, and I caught a glimpse of him sprawled out on the back stoop, smoking a cigarette. My eyes darted to Father's face, but he was looking straight ahead, humming softly. I relaxed my grip on the door handle.

At Miss X's apartment, the first floor of an old white house on the edge of campus, I climbed into the backseat and Father bounced up to her door. He rang the bell twice. Miss X appeared in the doorway, dressed in black lace-up shoes and a poop-colored satiny dress that looked like an old nightgown of Mother's. With Father at her side, she hobbled down the walk, already yacking away, punching the ground with her cane, scowling like she was ready to bite someone. Her bangs were too short, hacked off near the top of her forehead.

Father opened the car door and she heaved herself into the front seat, slouching down till she could barely see over the dashboard. The smell of cigarettes and face powder seemed to settle over everything.

Without acknowledging my presence, she continued her tirade. "And her obituary was in the *New York Times*. An entire page, wasted. The woman was a fraud, I'm telling you, Marshall. Did you know she was my roommate at Smith? Her family was dirt poor, but she lied about it. Like she did about everything."

Father winked at me in the rearview mirror, where I sat, stunned and hungry for more.

We started toward home and Miss X kept on, seemingly oblivious to where she was and where she was going. She might have been riding along on the Siberian railroad, addressing the passengers at large. I tried desperately to think of something to say, something to show her that she and I were on the same side, or could be. When she paused for breath, I blurted out, "Who are you talking about?" My voice sounded foolish and thin.

"Miss X," Father said, "this is my daughter, Jane."

Miss X did not turn around. "She wouldn't know her," she said to Father, soothingly, as though she were in the company of simpletons. She started in again, in her raspy voice, like she'd never been interrupted. "A two-faced bitch, that one. Her autobiography is full of lies. God! The woman strings words together like plastic beads. Oh, but the critics eat it up. Like they do any trash. You just wait. When I die, they won't devote a paragraph to me. It's a goddamn disgrace."

Back at home, Mother busied herself in the kitchen while Miss X, Father, and I trouped into the living room. Father and I perched on chairs facing Miss X, who sank down into the center of the couch, looking like a decadent elf. She had bright spots of rouge on her cheeks, and dark pouches under her watery blue eyes. She held forth on various topics, all relating to herself, drank four gin and tonics Mother brought in to her, and smoked six cigarettes down to the nubs. Father would get up every so often to poke the fire in the wood-burning stove. Occasionally I would ask her a question, no longer hoping for an alliance, but still trying to make my presence known. She would either ignore me or cover her mouth and giggle. Finally she said to Father, in a conspiratorial whisper, "Doesn't she know any better?"

I stomped up to my room and slammed the door. So she was going to treat me like an idiot child. We would see about that. I changed into tight jeans and a black scoop-neck top, my boyfriend's favorite outfit. I fastened my hair in a knot at the nape of my neck, and dipped into the secret stash of makeup I'd hidden in an old Whitman's Sampler box and shoved under my bed. I got to work on my face—brushing on brown eye shadow, blending it in, rubbing some off, applying a little more, rubbing some off, until Mother called me for dinner. Before I went downstairs, I made sure they couldn't tell I had any on at all.

We ate at the dining room table, with the white linen table-cloth and stiff linen napkins, the white china, navy blue candles in the brass candleholders. A Bach Brandenburg Concerto was playing in the background. Outside, it was dark.

Mother and Father sat at their ends of the table. Mother wore the Indian sari she saved for special occasions. I sat on one side of the table, Miss X on the other. Miss X was hunched over in her chair. She would take a bite of beef burgundy and then, with a shaking, clawlike hand, reach for her wine glass.

She talked to Father, but out of the corner of her eye, for the first time that evening, she was watching me. I stared back until she blinked and looked away.

"Marshall," she said. "Did I ever tell you about the time I had dinner with Mayor Lindsay?"

"No, don't believe so," Father said, helping himself to the creamed carrots. I could tell by his fixed smile that he'd heard this story many times.

Mother chewed slowly.

I started gobbling my food, but after three mouthfuls I was full.

"Let me tell you," Miss X said, peering at me again. "Mayor Lindsay. We were having dinner together, after a reading, a group of us, at Tavern on the Green. I ended up sitting next to the mayor. The man didn't remember that I was a poet, if you can imagine that. Thought I was one of the wives. What an ass. And I'd always respected him. Even voted for him."

"Can I be excused?" I said, rolling my eyes at Mother.

Mother ignored me.

Miss X grunted. "Anyway, it was a group of us at the Tavern on the Green, those of us who'd read at City College that evening, you understand. For some reason they'd put me first on the program, which infuriated me . . ."

"I said, can I be excused?"

Miss X sniffed and took a gulp of wine. I was getting to her, I could tell.

"You're not finished with your dinner," Mother said, like I was three years old.

"I'm not hungry anymore."

"Don't be rude," Father said, frowning at me.

Miss X pursed her lips, vindicated. "Excellent meal, Shirley," she said, not even looking at Mother. "Now, as I was saying . . ."

"I have to go. I've got a date." I'd been saving this till the right moment, but as soon as I'd said it I wished I hadn't.

"*She's* old enough?" Miss X covered her mouth and giggled in her hissing way, like a leaking tire.

Mother smiled at me. "Jane's boyfriend is such a nice young man."

"Come on, Mother."

"I can imagine," Miss X said, nodding.

"They don't really date," Mother said. "His brother drives them into town for ice cream." She reached over and patted my hand.

My ears began to burn.

"Is that so?" Miss X said. A sly look came over her face. "Are you sure?" She leaned toward Mother and said in a loud whisper, "They start early these days, you know."

I glanced quickly at Mother and Father, but Mother was staring down at her plate, and Father was pouring himself more wine. Miss X narrowed her eyes at me, and I felt like she could see me and my boyfriend together.

She shook her finger. "Better keep tabs on this one, Marshall. She'll do everything you tell her not to. Twice."

I wrinkled my nose at her.

She sat up straight, self-righteous, her cheeks as red as the wine. "Mark my words. That child's no more a virgin than I am."

I gasped, trying to appear outraged. "How would you know?"

Mother and Father locked eyes.

My skin prickled all over. "You don't know what you're talking about," I said.

"Jesus God." Miss X wadded her napkin and threw it on the table. "Young people these days have absolutely no manners."

"You don't have such hot manners yourself."

Father dropped his fork on his plate. "All right. You're not going anywhere tonight. You're grounded."

"What for? It's her fault."

"You'd better apologize, missy," Miss X said. Her lips looked like they'd been pulled tight with a drawstring. "Nobody talks to me like that and gets away with it."

Mother cleared her throat. "I'm sure Jane didn't mean . . ."

Miss X jerked around. "Shut your face, woman."

Mother shrank back in her chair. She turned toward me,

and her expression was one I'd never seen before—vulnerable, exposed.

My eyes blurred with tears. "You shut yours," I said. I was shaking all over. I stumbled out of my chair, raced over to the staircase, and leaped up the stairs two at a time. "You old witch!" I shrieked over my shoulder.

Miss X beat on the table with her fists. "She can't talk to me that way!" she wailed. "She can't talk to me that way. I'm a famous poet!"

I lay on my bed, sobbing, sure that my life would end now that I'd spoken that way to an adult. To a famous poet. I heard Father and Miss X go out the back door and Mother begin washing the dishes, banging the pots and pans even more loudly than usual. My sobs subsided and I looked around my room—at the low dormer ceiling which never allowed me to stand up straight, the frayed Oriental rug, my white dresser and vanity, snapshots of my friends around the mirror. None of it looked familiar.

I thought about my boyfriend, the one who was expecting me at that very minute. He'd be furious, and would probably break up with me. It was over. I repeated this to myself a few times, and tried to tell myself I was sad, but underneath I knew I was relieved. In his familiarity he'd become faintly repulsive—his slobbery kisses, his bleached hair and flannel shirts, his foul mouth, his pale butt, his spindly little penis.

The next morning I didn't wake up until ten, and then I lay in bed, afraid to go downstairs. They might still be furious about the way I'd behaved. I remembered how Miss X had pointed her finger and accused me. Mother and Father might've talked last night and agreed that I was bad, and that things were going to change.

I could think of only one way to handle it. I hopped out of bed and padded into their bedroom, and pawed through Mother's dresser until I found her old poop-colored nightgown; rooted a pair of black wing-tips from Father's closet; and snatched up his walking stick, which was leaning in the corner. Back in my room, I put on the nightgown and the shoes, smeared red lipstick on my cheeks, and, with my mascara wand, drew black circles under my eyes. I crept downstairs and slipped into my eavesdropping spot near the kitchen door—a space between the hutch and the wall.

Mother was talking on the phone. From her long silences, I knew she was talking to the poet. "What? Today? No, I'm busy. Marshall's busy too. I'm sorry too." She hung up.

"Can you believe her?" Now she was talking to Father, who was probably sitting at the kitchen table, drinking his fifth cup of coffee. Mother scooted a chair out. "The gall of that woman. 'Shirley, an old friend of mine, a poet, you've heard of him?' Of course I hadn't. 'He's coming into the airport in Indianapolis this afternoon, and I was wondering if you could pick him up?' That's it. I'm washing my hands of her."

Father had no reply.

I breathed in the familiar Sunday morning smells of pancakes and coffee, and watched the seconds tick by on the wall clock, waiting for them to say something else, maybe something about how rude Miss X had been to me, how sorry they were.

Finally Father broke the silence. "Have I told you who we're getting next year? Someone really good. Fellow from South Africa."

I couldn't stand it any longer. Heart pounding, I tottered into the kitchen, tapping the walking stick on the floor. "Hello, Marshall," I growled.

Father set down his newspaper and gripped his flannel robe over his chest. "Well. Good morning."

"Pancakes?" Mother said. She seemed to sink down into her puffy white bathrobe, which enveloped her like a sleeping bag. There was a book of poetry beside her plate. She speared her last bite of pancakes, swirled it in syrup, and popped it into her mouth.

I shook my fist in the air and bellowed, "How dare you? I'm a famous poet."

Father gave a nervous snort, picked up his newspaper, shook it, and started reading.

"Would you like some pancakes?" Mother said, her eyebrows knitting together. She was looking right at me, but it was like she couldn't see me.

Deflated, I propped the stick against the wall. "No thanks," I said, my tone matter-of-fact, like theirs. "I'll have cereal."

Mother's face relaxed. She said, in a kinder voice, "Are you sure?"

I nodded, sat down at the table, and stared at a coffee stain on the white linoleum floor. I realized that they were right—pretending it had never happened was easiest. It seemed I was going to come out of this unscathed. I might not even be grounded. I thought about going to see my boyfriend, trying to make some excuse about last night, but I couldn't even picture his face clearly anymore. Right then I began thinking of other boys I knew, trying to conjure up a new face, one that belonged to someone even more daring and wicked than my old boyfriend, and I came up with a few possibilities. Of course, I had no idea then that this was only the beginning, that my search would continue, year after year, long after I knew how dangerous it was, long after I wanted to stop. But at that moment, I thought I was off the hook. Even so, I couldn't resist giving Mother a final Miss X scowl.

Mother quickly lowered her eyes. She opened her book, flipped through the pages, stopped, smoothed the book open, and began reading a poem out loud, softly, to herself.

BlesSing

T H E   D A Y after New Year's, late in the afternoon, Riley gives in to himself and decides to go looking for arrowheads. He invites his son Matt, who is stretched out on the living room couch, to come with him. He makes the outing sound as enticing as possible, mentioning exercise, fresh air, history, and artifacts.

"Whatever," Matt mumbles from under his red, white, and blue afghan. *The Sun Also Rises* slides off the leather couch and plops on the carpet. Matt, a junior at IU, is home for Christmas break. He goes out every night with his high school sweetheart, Heather, and then naps all day.

Riley taps a rolled map against his thigh, waiting, till Matt pokes his head out, glaring at Riley like he's a stranger. Finally Matt kicks the afghan aside and stands up, a head taller than his father. He stretches. "Let's take Kip," he says, yawning.

Just back from aerobics, Riley's wife Marlene and Heather are settled at the kitchen table, clipping articles from magazines and filing them in manila folders. Heather's helping Marlene with a project for her master's thesis—a national survey of farm wives to discover how they've coped with the farm crisis. Heather fits right into their family, better than their own daughter ever has.

"We're going on an expedition," Riley announces as he and Matt come into the kitchen.

Marlene, in her velour sweatsuit, flips off her reading glasses and lets them fall on the chain around her neck. "To that Indian village, I bet."

According to the historical map Marlene gave Riley for Christmas, the site of what once was the largest Indian settlement in Indiana is just ten miles from their farm.

"Boys only?" Heather asks Matt, her scissors dangling open. Heather's striped leotard molds her body. Her dark hair twirls in shiny corkscrews. Matt whispers in Heather's ear, then kisses her twice on the lips.

"Need to take provisions?" Marlene asks Riley over the rim of her coffee mug.

"We'll be back in a couple hours for dinner." Riley bends down and pecks her cheek.

Marlene picks up her stack of folders and taps them on the table to straighten them. "Don't look too hard, or you won't find one."

Riley's been looking for arrowheads since he was a boy walking beans on his grandfather's farm in Iowa. When he and his father hunted pheasant along Wildcat Creek, Riley scanned the banks for arrowheads. With Marlene, he searched the Arizona desert on a cross-country trip in '67. At age forty-nine, while disking his fields, Riley still keeps an eye out. So far, he hasn't found one.

Many times Riley has imagined the moment—a chiseled

tip poking up through the earth, his hand reaching out. Finding an arrowhead has come to mean the same thing as having a vision—being singled out for something important. But he can't explain this to anyone.

"If we don't look, we damn sure won't find one," he says.

Marlene slips her glasses back on. "Well, that's true." Then, as Riley's closing the door behind them, she calls, "How's the Beef House sound for dinner?"

Matt drives his Accord, a high school graduation present. Riley sits beside him, feeling bulky and clumsy. Kip presses his muzzle against the back window. They bounce down gravel roads between velvet black fields, then turn north on Division Highway, which after five miles becomes River Road. The sky curving over them is cloudless, Dutch blue.

"Great weather," Riley says. "First day the sun's been out in a month. Not one inch of snow yet this year. But then last year we didn't get a good one till February. Maybe the atmosphere's heating up. I read that somewhere. Greenhouse effect."

"It snowed it Bloomington," Matt says. He's frowning at the tape deck, punching fast forward, letting out blurts of music, then fast forwarding again.

A man on a motorcycle putters up beside them. Matt reaches for the tape box and their car drifts toward the cyclist. Matt looks up and pulls the wheel back. The man gives them the finger and accelerates.

"Guy belongs in a nuthouse," Riley says, gripping the door handle.

"Does Mom ever come up for air?"

"Once in a while. She's busier now than she's ever been. Here's the turn."

Matt downshifts and swings left onto a rutted gravel road. "We used to come out here," he shouts over the music and the rocks flipping against the undercarriage. "Back in high school."

Riley turns down the music. "What?"

"Never mind." On both sides of the road, yellow prairie grass lies flat, matted down by frost. As they creak over the wooden planks of Granville Bridge, Riley looks down through rusty iron bars at the Wabash. Muddy water swirls under them, sweeping along chunks of ice like giant blobs of wax.

Riley has a print of Bingham's *Fur Traders Descending the Missouri* in his den. In his mind, they're descending the Wabash. He belts out, "Through the sycamores the candle-light is gleaming, on the banks of the Wabash, far away . . ." He waits for Matt to join in. Matt was in the Glee Club in high school. But now he keeps silent, staring straight ahead, and Riley trails off, self-conscious.

They clank off the bridge, pass the chalky white sycamores lining the bank, and start uphill between two fields of dry corn husks.

"I heard that's a top-notch bird spot." Riley points up ahead to a grove of trees, purple against the sky. "Let's bring Kip out here next fall. He misses you." Riley reaches back and scratches Kip's ear. Kip's tail thumps at the sound of his name.

"Wish I had more weekends free. I do miss hunting. Did you go this year?"

"Not once." Riley tries to sound casual, but fails. He reasserts himself. "Why don't we pull off here? Right here's where the Indian village was. The Wea Plain. We can walk along the edge of these fields a ways."

"You got it, Patches." Last summer Matt found pictures of Riley, pictures Riley kept in the bottom of the file cabinet and hadn't even shown Marlene. Bathing suits, beer, women. And Riley with bushy black sideburns—patches.

Riley grabs the back of Matt's neck and squeezes.

"Cut it out." Matt elbows Riley.

For a moment Riley feels twenty years lighter. "Park!"

"Yes, sir!" Matt wheels over onto the left side of the road. They climb out, hunching their shoulders in the cold air. Riley opens the back door for Kip, who leaps out and sniffs furiously around the front tire.

Matt zips up a light windbreaker over the football letter sweater he borrowed from Riley. The knees of his thin army pants ripple in the wind. "Which way?"

"Well, let's see." Riley swivels on the heel of his workboot. "The Indian camp went both ways along the river here." He pauses for effect. "But let's go right. With the wind, since you didn't dress warm."

Matt whirls and stalks off across the field, Kip trotting beside him.

"This is like hitchhiking in a snowstorm," Riley says as he catches up to them. "Your destination changes with the way the wind is blowing."

Matt knits his thick eyebrows together and scrunches his mouth to one side. "Weird," his face says.

"Let's go to the top of this field and look along the edge," Riley says. "The Indians farmed four hundred acres of squash and corn here. We might find all sorts of things. Who knows?"

"Who knows?"

Turning right, they walk uphill, stepping over the furrows. Kip weaves between them, tail waving like a metronome. Wind numbs the inch of flesh between Riley's Pioneer Seed cap and his scarf. He wriggles snugly in his thermal underwear. He notices that Matt's naked ears, under his spiked black hair, glow pink.

At the top of the field they curve left, walking parallel to the river, hidden by woods three hundred yards below them. A string of maple trees on their right separates this field from the next field up. They stop to look between the trees at a white two-story farmhouse which is nearly identical to theirs. "Whose land is this?" Matt asks.

"Belongs to the head of IBM. He bought up the riverfront land this side of Granville Bridge clear up to Lilly's, as an investment. Along here should be a good place for arrowheads." Riley squats down, picking at a rock with his gloved fingers.

They creep along, bent over, scanning the ground. The corn here, like that on Riley's land, has been plowed under. The soil is sandy—brown flakes frosted with ice crystals. Riley tugs at a rock frozen in the ground. He stamps his foot. It's like stamping on iron. He kicks the rock, a flint he'd hoped at first was an arrowhead. His big toe stings. He should have waited till spring.

Riley had mentioned the Indian village to Marlene's brother, Simms, while they were dawdling over coffee one morning at the Grand Prairie Cafe. Simms gave advice, as usual. "Spring's the best time to look. Thaw'll bring arrowheads to the surface."

But Riley couldn't wait till spring. He sold the hogs two years ago. They'd canceled their annual trip to Orlando because of Marlene's classes, and all that's on his schedule is church-league basketball.

"These things are really in there," Matt says, chipping away at the dirt with a stick.

Riley decides he and Matt should talk about something important. Marlene'll want a report tonight. Matt's their quiet child, the one who keeps his distance. Not like their daughter, Lynn, a potter in Nags Head, who tells them more than they want to know.

"How's school?" Riley's eyes mechanically sweep the ground.

"Better than being slapped in the face with a wet fish, I guess."

"Where you gonna apply to law school?"

"Don't know."

"Hmmm." Getting Matt to talk seriously about himself is like prying these rocks out of the ground.

"What kind of Indians lived here, anyway?" Matt asks.

"Middle Mississippian. Then Miami and Potawatami. This is the only place in the country where Plains, Mississippian, and Algonquin Indians came together," Riley says, realizing he took the bait.

They examine pink rocks, gray ones, rusty brown ones. Riley has a sinking feeling he won't find an arrowhead today— that he might never find one.

Last year Simms tried to give Riley a shoebox full of projectile points, knives, and scrapers he'd found on his Warren County farm. "From the prehistoric Middle Mississippian culture," Simms had said, worrying an arrowhead in his worm-colored fingers.

"I can tell that. Thanks, but keep 'em," Riley said. Simms couldn't understand the importance of finding them yourself.

"How come you quit going to church?" Matt says.

"Haven't."

"You didn't go today."

"Don't like the new minister. I'm taking a leave of absence."

"He's a redneck." Matt crouches on his haunches, his breath puffing out like cigarette smoke. "I can't say that to Mom. She'd have a shit fit."

"Okay, bud, enough." Riley sounds firmer than he feels. He remembers the Sunday last month he'd sat in the congregation because he'd missed choir rehearsal. Three pews ahead sat Dawn, the minister's wife. Riley marveled at the fact that her neck could have been any neck. It evoked no memory of the evening he and Dawn had spent in the church lounge with the door locked. That was the first time Riley had ever acted on the familiar impulse. It had been an attempt to capture something that was never there, and he assumed Dawn knew the same.

As they stood to sing the benediction, Riley watched Marlene singing with her shoulders thrown back, breasts straining against the scarlet choir robe. Their eyes met, and Marlene's lips bloomed in a smile. Riley smiled back.

During the postlude when he turned to leave, Riley felt Dawn staring at him. She blocked one end of his pew, so he edged out the other end. He hasn't been back to church since then.

Matt and Riley approach the end of the field, now walking briskly. They brush through a grove of saplings, bare branches whipping their faces, and into a clearing. Logs form a circle in the dry leaves, as if someone planned to make a bonfire and forgot. Riley plops down on a log. His neck aches from looking at the ground.

"Wanna keep going? I'm plenty warm," Matt says, hopping on one foot and then the other, bare ankles flashing. His cheeks are flushed.

"Sure. Hey, where's Kip?" Riley jumps up. He fights down a wave of panic, the same way he did when the kids got lost at the state fair. "Kip! Here Kipper!" He cups his hands around his mouth and yells in every direction.

Matt does the same. "Kip! Here boy!"

Kip's barking, faint but ecstatic, comes from the river.

"He's swimming," Matt says, and smiles at Riley.

"We'd better go get him."

They set off out of the grove and start down a soybean field toward the river.

"Does he swim much?" Matt asks.

"No. Never thought of bringing him here. Not that I have the time."

"He'd love it."

"Feel free."

"Sorry. Just a suggestion."

Kip belongs to both of them. The summer after Matt's junior year in high school, Riley, Marlene, and Matt went to visit Lynn and Sara in their beach cottage. Riley and Matt spent hours throwing a stick for Sara's Chesapeake Bay Retriever. They loved his red kinky coat and little pig eyes, and they loved the fact that his ancestors swam to the Eastern Shore of Virginia after a shipwreck, origins unknown.

Riley and Matt decided they should have a Chesapeake. That winter they studied breeders' information, and in March they drove to the Eastern Shore for their puppy. They named him Kiptopeke, after the town he was born in.

As they near the bottom of the field, the muddy river smell rises up to meet them. The earth becomes wetter and softer, and the wind dies down.

"Hey," Matt says. He scrapes his deck shoe along a row of dried bean plants.

"Yes?"

"Are you and Mom down about Lynn and Sara?"

"No. We don't think about it. Why?"

"Just checking."

Riley realizes he's grinding his teeth, something the dentist warned him against. He relaxes his jaw. "Don't say that to your mom. Kip!" Riley calls, and Kip woofs in reply.

They enter the woods where the remnants of the Wabash and Erie Canal, now a line of unconnected ditches, lie between them and the river. Riley picks his way through the underbrush, skirting a frozen ditch.

Matt stops at the ditch, pushing down with one foot at the edge, testing. The ice cracks below the surface with a dull twang. "Hey, you could skate on these babies," he yells.

Riley turns around to see Matt inching his way onto the ice. "That's not gonna hold you."

Matt steps back to the bank and picks up a rock. He sends it skittering over the ice, making a hollow ringing sound. "Cool."

Riley continues around the ditch, pressing on toward the river, pushing aside the brittle cane towering above his head, crunching cattails beneath his feet.

"Yoo-hoo!" Matt is sidling across the trunk of a tree hanging across the ditch, as if he's walking a tightrope. He waves at Riley, then gyrates to keep his balance. Riley imagines Matt falling, the way he fell off the gate when he was three and had to have five stitches in his forehead. Riley turns away.

When he reaches the riverbank, Riley steps between the sycamore trees. Kip is swimming in circles, fighting the current, yipping and splashing. His breath steams in a cloud over his head.

Riley feels his shoulders loosen. Kip is a born swimmer. Swimming is one thing he didn't have to be taught. Riley remembers the day he and Matt went to visit Kip at the training camp in Virginia. They watched Kip retrieve dummies from an unmowed field, then walked him back to the kennel with the trainer. The dogs in the kennel stopped barking instantly when the trainer said, "Quiet."

"Wow! How'd you teach 'em that?" Matt said.

"The pens are electric," the trainer said. "They learn."

Riley glanced at his son, wishing Matt hadn't asked. Matt's eyes darted to Riley's face, then away. He jerked around and began stroking the nose of a black Lab through a metal gate. "Good boy, good boy," he said.

Matt pops up beside Riley on the riverbank. "Kip's having the time of his life," he says, panting.

"I'll try to take him swimming once in a while."

They sit down on the hard ground together. Beginning at their toes, paper-thin sheets of ice slope down toward the river where the water has receded. Riley breaks off a piece, imprinted with the outline of a leaf. He flicks his wrist and the ice shatters on the rocks with a tinkling sound. From the lower branches of the sycamore trees, icicles hang in uniform rows like the candles Marlene makes at Christmas. On the opposite bank is the town of Riverview. A grain elevator, then railroad tracks, then a church and two rows of houses huddled together, as if for protection against the river and the prairie. In a mud lot beside the grain elevator sits a row of identical white trailers, each with a different color trim—red, blue, yellow. The smell of burning trash drifts over the water.

"Can you keep a secret?" Matt says.

Riley knows this is something else he doesn't want to hear. "I'll try."

Matt's chewing the inside of his cheek, a habit he picked up from Marlene. "Heather and I are engaged."

"You're too young," Riley says, then wishes he'd thought first.

"We're not getting married till next summer."

"I mean can't you wait till you finish school? Till you know what you want?" The picture of Matt and Heather living together, playing house, is almost as upsetting as that of Lynn and Sara in their beach cottage.

"Heather's the one thing I'm sure of," Matt says, cracking an ice sheet with his heel. "You and Mom got married when you were in college."

"I'd been in the Navy four years," Riley says, knowing it hadn't made any difference in his marriage. "When will you tell your mother?"

"Tonight. I want your blessing, Dad." The words sound stilted coming from Matt.

A flash of white on the opposite bank catches Riley's eye. A hawk floats up from the brush, then begins slowly pumping its wings. A string of red entrails swings from its beak.

"Matt." Riley points at the hawk, now disappearing over some trees, blackened and backlit by the setting sun.

"You and Mom are happy."

"Uh-huh."

"We'll live in married student housing. We'll both work

and go to school part-time. When we graduate, we want to go out West. Like you two did."

The cold is seeping up through Riley's pants. He stands and gives Matt a hand up. "Let's go."

Without calling for Kip, they walk back through the trees at an angle, toward the car. Riley hears Kip paddle to the shore, shake himself, and thrash through the cane after them. They come upon an abandoned trailer, its moss-green paint still showing between rust spots.

"Did someone actually live in this?" Matt asks.

"Maybe used it for a fishing camp."

"Strange." Matt slumps on ahead, his hands in his pockets, suddenly looking ten years older.

Riley examines the empty shell of the trailer—the rotting wooden floor, rusty smokestack, ladder propped against the side—as if searching for an explanation.

"Look." Matt bends down beside a tree, where Kip is sniffing at something.

Riley crosses over to them. Small silvery fish, like half dollars with black filmy eyes, are papered against the bottom and sides of a dried puddle. "Got caught when the river went down," he says. He pokes at one, the belly spongy and the tail stiff, frozen to the ground. "They're either little crappies or sunfish. I'll look 'em up when we get home."

Matt straightens up and backs away. "I really don't expect you to have all the answers."

They tramp on through the woods. Riley wraps his arm around Matt's shoulders. "It's just that we worry about you, okay?"

"I know," Matt says. "I worry about you, too."

They walk out into the field. A thin mist, like steam, swirls over the ground. In the middle of the field is a frozen puddle as big as a pond. Matt lopes toward it. He stomps along the edge, making little puddles. Kip trails him, slurping up the water.

Riley steps onto the ice, gingerly at first. His stomach

lurches when his right boot slips through with a crunch. Farther out, the ice is bubbled but solid. Riley begins to slide, first slowly, then he runs to build up speed. He sails down the length of the puddle. "Come on out, Matt." Wind whips the words from his mouth.

He turns to see Matt standing in the center of the puddle, watching him. Matt begins to tap-dance, knocking his heels and toes on the ice, spinning in circles.

Riley runs as fast as he can toward Matt, then lunges and slides, leaning into it. "Whooo!"

Matt is bent double, laughing. He holds out his arms to protect himself. Riley, still sliding, crouches down and bear-hugs Matt's knees. Matt flops on top of Riley and they roll over and over on the ice, pretending to wrestle. Then they untangle themselves and collapse flat on their backs, still heaving with laughter. Kip crouches, rump hiked up, barking.

"Well, it's getting dark," Riley finally says. "We'd better head back."

But they lie side by side, staring up at the now pale sky, rippling with gray-peaked clouds, like waves.

"I've got an arrowhead if you want one," Matt says. "Found it detasseling last year."

"Thanks, son."

The wind groans in the trees, and Riley feels sweat freezing on his neck. He sits up, leaning back on his hands. Below the clouds, Venus glows like a silver bead in dark blue sky, and below that, the gold light warms to apricot. Smoke curls up from black roofs in Riverview. Riley thinks of his split oak, stacked neatly beside the stove at home. Bells twang out, tinny and hollow, from a church across the river.

"What's that hymn?" Matt says, lifting his head. He starts humming.

Riley listens. The tune is familiar, one that he has heard all of his life. He tries to think of the words, but he can't remember them. Instead he begins to hum softly, along with Matt.

Plywood Rabbit

"DARCE," MOM calls, first thing, when she comes in. Checking up on me. She manages Foxmoor Casuals at the mall, and tonight she worked till nine.

I punch off the TV and scoot Brandy into my lap.

Mom drags herself into the living room, where Brandy and I are sitting on the floor, and flops down in her rocking chair. She slides her feet half out of her high heels and clacks the pointed toes together.

"A-B-C," I say, holding Brandy's finger over a page of the alphabet book. We were actually watching a "Magnum" rerun before she came in, and Brandy doesn't understand the switch. She's two and a half years old. Mom treats me like I'm two and a half, instead of twenty-two.

She lights a cigarette, fans out the match, and

says, "Don't you know a thing about child development? You're frustrating her."

As if on cue, Brandy screws up her face and whines.

"What a day. Inventory." She tilts back her head and out comes a stream of smoke.

"She was fine till you came in." I swing Brandy up into my arms. Brandy doesn't like fighting, that's what it is. I carry her into my bedroom, where I can at least lock the door.

The next morning at six, while I'm in the bathroom curling my hair and drinking coffee, I plot my strategy. Mom's threatening to file for custody of Brandy. We go to the welfare office tonight for counseling. Mom called up last week and made an appointment, thinking, I suppose, that a social worker could talk sense into me. I agreed to go, but Mom's the one who needs some sense talked into her. I've put on my good jeans and white sweater, but my hair flips up instead of back and I have to keep plastering it with hairspray to make it mind. By the time I get into Brandy's room I'm choking on hairspray fumes. Mom's already snuck in to dress Brandy.

"I'll take care of my child."

"Says you." Mom pulls a purple T-shirt that says I ❤ BERMUDA over Brandy's head. She got it on a singles' cruise last February. A sign of her devotion.

"She'll freeze her butt off in that skimpy thing."

"I know." She yanks a sweatshirt on Brandy, then runs the brush through her hair like she's grooming a dog.

"Maaa," Brandy wails, her big dark eyes pleading with me.

"I'm here, hon." I slip purple sneakers on Brandy's feet. "I'm sure glad you're so concerned all of a sudden," I say, breaking my promise to myself not to egg her on.

Mom rears back and slaps her hands on her hips. "You've got some nerve. After all I've done for you." She sticks her face right up in my face. Her pink satin robe stinks of cigarettes.

I snatch up Brandy's windbreaker, bag, and then Brandy. "That's it, run away. Like you always do."

Brandy goes to day care, even though it takes most of my paycheck. The rest I'm saving. Her sitter lives at the other end of town, but it's only four blocks away, which tells you the size of Green Hill. When the weather's nice, we walk.

The oak leaves along Main are red, and the maple leaves are yellow at the tips. I hang my head back and wish I could climb up and be surrounded by all that color. I pick a red leaf for Brandy and she waves it like a flag. We walk past Fuller Hardware, the Nite Owl Tavern, and the Monon Funeral Home. All dark this early in the morning. I slip out of my jean jacket, knot it around my waist, and think about the fall afternoons, back when I was in high school, when I'd stretch out on Mom's front-porch swing underneath the honeysuckle vines, drink Pepsi, and watch the swimming-pool-blue sky going on forever. I dreamed of freedom, counting the days till graduation when I could leave Indiana forever. But as you can see, I never got very far.

I work at the Green Hill IGA, and I'm the only checker during the day, but it's never real busy. It's a small store, just four aisles and a meat counter in back. We sell almost everything that the Payless in town does. Our prices are a tad higher, of course. The floor is dirty brown linoleum squares, and the whole place smells like soggy carrots, but it's homey to me.

This morning I unlock the store and sign my time card seven o'clock, close enough, tie on my green apron, and sit behind the register on a folding chair. I have to stand up now and then to ring up donuts for slit-eyed men heading for the early shift, but even then I think my own thoughts.

I think about Raymond and the case Mom'll make against me, even though she thought Brandy's daddy was the greatest when she met him. On the night of June 27, back when I was nineteen and working here, Raymond came through the checkout line with a few odds and ends and started sweet-talking me. He said he worked for a contracting company out of Anderson, laying pipe in Green Hill. He asked me if he could come see me later, and I was so shocked I said, "Why not?" After that he came over every night and charmed us. Mom called him our *Playgirl* centerfold. I didn't think much of him drinking three sixes a night then. Now I know better.

Toward noon, business picks up, and then at three Scott Brooks comes in. He's a senior in high school and works the meat counter every afternoon. Tom Cruise with blond hair, sort of. He fishes in the pocket of his letter jacket and pulls out a rabbit the size of my hand. It's flat and wooden, varnished with shellac. There's a pink bow painted around its neck, and its eyes, nose, and whiskers are painted in black. BRANDY is painted in white letters on the body.

"All the guys think Brandy's my secret squeeze. Made it in shop." He gives it to me and struts on toward the back, humming.

"Thanks." I don't know what else to say. I run my fingers over the rabbit, so smooth and shiny. Over the word BRANDY. For the first time it hits me that I might lose her. To my own mother.

When the bell on the door tinkles, I wipe my eyes quick and set the rabbit next to the register. Delyte Gutwein strolls in. Even though it's fifty degrees out she's wearing a fiber-filled coat. Her hair is bouffed out like marshmallows and dyed orange. Delyte owns Mane Street Beauty Salon, which supposedly makes her better than everyone else.

She ignores me, grabs a cart, and heads for the chips and dip. I look at Scott, leaning on the metal meat counter in his white apron with blood spots on it. He makes circles with his index finger beside his head and grins. To keep from laughing, I walk over and rearrange the Campbell's Soup cans.

"Darcy, where'd you get this?" Delyte crows.

I hurry back to the checkout. She's bent over, examining Brandy's rabbit. "A friend made it," I say, businesslike, ringing up her Squirt and Little Debbie Figaroos.

"Who?" Delyte picks the rabbit up. "I bet I could sell these out of the shop."

I stick her junk in two paper sacks. "It's one of a kind." I lift the rabbit gently from between Delyte's claws and slip it into my pocket.

"Sheesh!" Delyte's eyebrows pop up like burnt toast. She purses her lips, stares at me hard, then grabs up the sacks. The bell above the door keeps on jingling after she leaves.

Scott and I are alone in the store. "The rabbit's for good luck tonight," Scott says. "Don't worry. You'll do fine."

He's sweet. I can tell him anything. But there's no way I'd rob the cradle that bad, though it's tempting. Lord, it's tempting.

At five-forty-five I'm exhausted. My ancient Toyota and I putter down 52 toward Green Hill. I'm coming back from my English class at Vo-Tech. My teacher, this prissy guy with a beard, didn't like my first essay. It was supposed to be a Personal Experience Essay, but he said it was too personal. It was about how when I followed Raymond back to Anderson I found out he was married and had two kids, I decided to hang around anyway. The teacher says I should write about things I have more distance from, whatever that means.

Pinpoints of light flicker in the farmhouses scattered across the prairie. Up ahead, the sun is sinking behind Green Hill. There's a row of clouds on the horizon that looks like mountains, a strip of dark red over them, a streak of purple, then a wash of pink. I look at the clouds and try to pretend they're real mountains. One day I'll see mountains. Raymond promised to take me to Aspen. He was always saying he wanted me to have the best—diamonds, a fur coat, trips to exciting places. Of course, he could never afford those things.

He would've been embarrassed to give me something corny like a plywood rabbit.

I stop by for Brandy and we pull up to the county welfare office at five till six. Mom's Ford is already in the parking lot. I carry Brandy up to the front door, more for my sake than hers. The welfare office used to be a roller rink, and I still expect disco lights and thumping music when I go in. Mom's standing in the lobby. A young woman with punked-out hair unlocks the door for me. Mom's all dressed up in a suit, looking like head honcho in charge. I wish I'd at least worn my black corduroys.

"This is Miss Clark," Mom says stiffly, nodding toward the punked-out woman.

"Alicia Clark. I'll be handling your case." She sticks out her hand for me to shake, which I do. She must be new here. She looks about my age. She's wearing a black dress with lime-green splashes on it. Her hair is shaved an inch above her ears and the rest hangs down in a bleached tail. I smirk at Mom, who sniffs and looks away. Things seem to be going my way already.

"Would you all come with me?" Alicia beckons us to follow her across the waiting room, and Mom does.

Brandy hides behind my legs, twisting a chunk of my thigh.

"Come on now, Bran," I say, although I don't blame her. I pull the rabbit out of my pocket, and realize I've been carrying it around all day, like a good memory or a favorite song. I give it to Brandy and let her hold it.

We follow Alicia and Mom down the long dim hallway. A Musak version of "Beat It" plays from speakers over our heads.

"This is our new counseling room," Alicia says, and opens a door at the end of the hall. She switches on lights. Everything is beige. On the back wall is a great big mirror. Two cameras are stuck up in the corners of the ceiling, like the kind in stores to catch shoplifters. A telephone with no dial hangs on the wall.

"Don't let this stuff bother you. I'll explain how we work in a sec. Just have a seat," Alicia says.

We all get settled in a circle, and right away Brandy wriggles out of my lap, still hanging on to her rabbit. She toddles over and sits down next to a box of toys in the corner.

"Brandy Ann, you come back here," I say, trying not to sound too bossy or mean. With welfare people you never know.

"That's okay, that's what those toys are there for," Alicia says. She's sitting next to me, bouncing a clipboard on her knee. She has three silver earrings in one ear. She explains that her supervisor will be watching us from behind the mirror, taping our session. She hands us a form to sign. I look at myself in the mirror and fix my bangs, quick, then glance around at the tacky nature posters on the wall. Something smells like BO.

"We're here today so you can get yourselves back on track as a family," Alicia says, glancing at both of us. "I'm here to give you a nudge now and then, but you'll be doing all the hard work."

Sounds like she memorized that one. Mom's not buying it either. We're both on the edge of our seats, ready to let go. This is a battle, and Alicia's going to decide who wins. Mom cuts her eyes at Alicia and flashes me a look like, "She doesn't know her head from a hole in the ground." But Mom wants Alicia on her side just like I do.

"What do we need to work on today?" Alicia's leaning forward in her chair. Nervous. She makes the mistake of looking too long at Mom, and Mom doesn't need a push to get started.

Mom starts in about Raymond and how I snuck off with him, which isn't true, I gave her a day's notice, and how I'm fixing to move out again, which I am, though I haven't told her yet, and how it's not fair to Brandy to be dragged all over creation and if I don't wake up and smell the coffee she'll get custody of Brandy and bring her up right. I break in and tell Alicia that speaking of unstable, Mom has no room to talk—she's been on and off welfare for years herself. I've never met my father. And where was all her concern when I was stuck in Anderson, pregnant and broke? Mom thought that if I would only act right, Raymond would come and rescue me.

Alicia is quiet, nodding, till the phone buzzes. She hops up to answer it. She listens a minute, hangs up, and sits back down. She says we don't want to dwell on the past and asks what the problem is now. Before I can answer, Mom butts in and says the problem is that I take advantage of her and go out drinking every night, which is a lie, I haven't been out in a month, so I point that out, but Mom ignores this and goes on about how irresponsible I am, which I once was, but not now, and I try to say so, but it's no use, because she's off on a tirade.

Brandy stops building her tower and stares at Mom.

Alicia chews on her lip and squirms. Then she blurts out, "Mrs. Bennett, Darcy's an adult and you're treating her like she's a child." Alicia's ears are red. She's taking this personally.

Mom stops talking and looks down at her purse, fiddling with the straps.

The phone buzzes again. Alicia leaps up to answer it. She listens for a few minutes, her face getting redder and redder. She turns her back on us and gently hangs up the phone. She sits down carefully in her chair, staring straight ahead, and takes a deep breath like she wishes we would disappear. Then she looks over at Mom and smiles, a wobbly smile. She slides her chair close to Mom's, puts her hand on Mom's shoulder, and leans close. "I think you're hurting right now."

Mom covers her face with her hands.

"Are you afraid?" Alicia asks, patting her.

Mom nods.

"Of what?"

"I don't want Darcy to end up like me." Her face is still covered and her voice is so quiet it scares me.

"Mom, what about your job? Your friends?"

She shakes her head.

I shouldn't say more, but I can't help it. "You went on that cruise to Bermuda. You had a great time."

She looks at me, a tear running down her cheek. "I didn't meet anyone."

She is never going to be happy, I realize, because she'll always find a reason not to be. She's always expected me to make her happy, but I can't, so I just squeeze her hand.

She squeezes back, and her eyes fly open like she just woke up. She slides her hand out from under mine and reaches into her purse, tugging out a Kleenex. "Well then," she says, dabbing her eyes. She stands up, twists her skirt straight, and squints at Alicia, then me. "Okay," she says, like we've just asked her for something. "Just forget the whole damn thing." She stalks out, slamming the door behind her.

Nobody else moves or says a word. My face in the mirror looks like an old friend I haven't seen in a while, and I'm thinking there's someone who will want to hear all about this.

In November Brandy and I get our own place, closer to town, a trailer in Pine Village Trailer Park. Scott and I are still friends. Well, more than friends. We go out on weekends, to a movie, to Wendy's, or to see Mom at Foxmoor. Mom's been cool and formal since she let down her guard at the welfare office, but she carries Brandy around, showing her off, when we visit her at the mall.

Scott's made Brandy lots of plywood animals since the rabbit. And some for me. An owl, a French poodle, a cow with a brass bell around its neck, a black cat. I keep them on Brandy's dresser. She only gets to play with one at a time. Her favorite's the cat. She twirls it by the tail.

We left the rabbit at the welfare office that night. When I went back the next day, it was gone. Scott hasn't made another rabbit, which is just as well, because that first rabbit really was one of a kind. Besides, it could do some good for whoever has it, if they realize what they've got. That's what I like to think, anyway.

Scavenger Hunt

HOME

I GOT the first clue in my fruit bowl. I was slouched over the kitchen table in my nightgown, scanning the *Journal*, and when I reached for my morning tangelo I found a pink plastic cigarette lighter in the shape of a pelican. Printed on the pelican's side were the words THE GRASS SHACK, a new restaurant in town, a place I'd never been. Somebody else had put the lighter in my fruit bowl. I knew this because I lived alone and ate fresh fruit every morning. I thumbed the wheel on the back of the pelican's head and a long wicked flame shot out, causing me to fling the lighter across the room, my heart pounding like I'd drunk a pot of coffee.

I stumbled out of my chair and clutched the edge of the sink, trying to calm myself. The view through the window was no consolation—November in Indiana, everything closing up shop. The sky looked greasy, and brown oak leaves lined the birdbath. The only spot of color in the yard was a little red picnic table where my son Bubbie used to eat his peanut butter sandwiches before he grew up to be a criminal. I hadn't seen Bubbie in two years. He couldn't come back home because he'd be arrested, but maybe the pelican in my fruit bowl was a message from him, delivered by one of his associates. Or maybe not. I tried to think logically. I hadn't noticed a break-in, but somebody could've come in through a basement window. No way was I going down there to find out. I turned on the hot water and started viciously scrubbing the breakfast dishes.

My house usually seemed spacious and comforting with its tall windows and wide doorways, framed school portraits of Bubbie on the walls, my antique clocks ticking away the days, but that morning there were too many dark nooks and big chairs behind which someone could crouch. I forced myself to start a load of laundry, all the while feeling like a bad actress feigning nonchalance on "Unsolved Mysteries." Last week they'd shown a segment about a young man who looked a little like Bubbie—Robert Stack called him Loverboy—who bilked vain old women out of their life savings. Bubbie's latest postcard came from San Diego, so I lay awake half the night imagining Bubbie sitting in a bar beside the San Diego Bay, his blond hair long and slicked back from his newly sophisticated face, toasting a wrinkled creature wearing a tennis visor.

Now, as I swept my kitchen floor, I could hear Robert Stack's melodramatic voice: "The morning began like any other for Francine Brick, until she made a bizarre discovery in her fruit bowl. It wasn't long before Francine realized that the pelican lighter was the signal she'd been waiting for." I dropped the broom and marched upstairs singing "She'll Be Coming Round the Mountain." In my dim bedroom I dug out some cheery, no-nonsense clothes, a corduroy skirt and a sweater with sunflowers all over it, something Bubbie had once given me for Christmas in hopes I'd turn into the type of person who'd wear such a thing. Now, oddly enough, the outfit gave me courage, like a uniform must do for a policewoman. When I was dressed I rushed downstairs, grabbed my purse and jacket, and dashed out the back door, slamming it behind me, trapping my sinister audience inside.

THE GRASS SHACK

I decided that whoever left the lighter wanted me to go to The Grass Shack, so I drove off toward its location on the outskirts of Lafayette, my knees shaking with reckless energy. For the first time in months I had a definite purpose, and I was relieved to be doing something, no matter how foolish, that might allow me to find out more about Bubbie. If Quentin, my ex-husband, were still around, he'd inform me once again that my elevator didn't go all the way to the top, and once again he'd trot out his evidence, reminding me that I used to suspect our neighbor of being a serial killer simply because he was single, cheerful, and always kept his shades down. He'd remind me of our Ozark vacation, when I spent an entire week with my ear pressed against the connecting door of the adjoining cabin, convinced that its occupants were perpetrating an insurance scam because they'd reported a valuable necklace stolen to the park rangers, and who would bring a valuable necklace on a float trip? But this situation was different, I'd tell Quentin, because it involved me directly and because I was plunging right into the thick of things. And I'd try to explain that all my life I'd been waiting for an opportunity like this to present itself, but someone like Quentin would never understand.

The Grass Shack was tucked back on a side street in an industrial park, a squat little building with a fake bamboo roof, a pink neon sign, and two cars in the parking lot. It was eleven o'clock, too early for lunch, but I decided to go in anyway. Inside it was cold and smelled like old broth. Dried starfish and sand dollars littered the walls, and hollowed-out blowfish hung from the ceiling, lit up inside by red bulbs. At first I didn't see anyone, and then, across the room, I noticed a man standing behind a bar shaped like the prow of a ship. "We're not open yet," he said. "Half an hour." I could only see him from the chest up. He was a short man with a long, baleful face, wearing a white apron and chef's hat.

I wanted to be direct, but not too direct. I said, "I've come about the lighter." He kept staring at me, and I sputtered out, "The pelican lighter. That says 'The Grass Shack' on it."

"The owner has one like that," the man said. "He had it special made."

So the owner was involved. Probably using The Grass Shack as a front for his shady activities. I took a few steps closer, my hands clenched in my jacket pockets. "Is he here? Can I talk to him?"

"No ma'am," the cook said. "He lives in Kokomo."

Kokomo was a dreary little factory town, just the sort of depressed and depressing place a gangster could easily get a foothold. "Could you give me his phone number?"

"What for, ma'am?"

I didn't know how much the cook knew about the pelican, but I decided to play dumb too. "I want to buy the lighter from him," I said. "Some friends and I have a contest going, to see who can collect the most unusual cigarette lighters." I batted my eyes at him. "We're a bunch of silly old ladies, you see."

"Har," he said. "We're not allowed to give out that information. Anyhow, the owner was in here last week and gave that lighter away to some lady. Not an old lady, though."

"Who? What's her name?"

"Can't remember. Works out at the mall. Dress shop, I think."

"What's she look like?"

"Dark hair. Wears speckled glasses." He shook his finger at me. "Don't let her buck teeth scare you."

"Takes more than buck teeth," I said, wondering if I was being threatened.

"Har," the man said again. "Good luck, ma'am." He turned and banged through some swinging doors into the kitchen.

I wandered back to my car, trying to appear unfazed, but my head was buzzing. I didn't know anyone who fit the cook's description, nor did I know anyone who worked at the mall. I hadn't been out there in years, not since Bubbie got into trouble. I wondered who the buck-toothed woman was and what she was up to. This was starting to seem like a nasty little game, just the sort of trick I'd love to play on someone else, and now I was getting a taste of my own medicine.

P R O P H E T' S   R O C K   M A L L

On Monday afternoons I usually went to pottery class, then to the library and the grocery store, but I decided to chuck it all and drive straight out to the mall. Since I'd last seen it, the mall had undergone some cosmetic changes—the orange benches, dark pools, and brown tile floors were gone, replaced by white tile, skylights, and large ficus trees—but the essence of the place was the same, a combination of fakery and boredom. When I walked past the SireShop, where Bubbie used to work, I looked straight ahead, feeling ashamed, as if I'd been the one caught stealing instead of Bubbie.

There were ten women's clothing stores in the mall, all carrying the same kind of cheaply made office-to-evening wear. Loud, repetitive pop music played in every store—"I'm going home I'm going home to your house I'm going home I'm going home . . ." I strolled around each store two or three times, fingering the Pre-Holiday Specials—slippery dresses and glittery sweaters—looking for someone who fit the cook's description, and discovered I was actually enjoying myself. My favorite job ever was one I'd had in college, when I'd worked as a secret shopper for a department store in Bloomington, pretending to be a customer and purchasing items with the store's money, then filling out reports on the salespeople. The salespeople soon caught on, since I kept buying Quad A shoes and returning them, and after that it wasn't much fun, but I still remembered some techniques I'd learned on that job, and I planned to use them on the buck-toothed woman, as soon as I found her.

I didn't find her. After checking out the last clothing store with no success, I bought a mocha and sat down at a round table in an imitation sidewalk cafe, feeling hollow with disappointment. Directly in front of me, with its walls of blue jeans, was the SireShop, brightly lit but totally empty of customers. I wondered who was managing the store now. When his friends went off to Purdue or Indiana University, Bubbie got his own apartment and stayed on at the SireShop, and after a couple of years he was promoted to manager. Quentin and I began to accept the fact that this was the kind of life our son might lead and that it wasn't such an awful thing. Then Bubbie was accused of stealing—money and clothes worth over ten thousand dollars. He pled guilty, and the judge let him off with parole, since he'd never been in trouble before. The money was gone, of course—he'd spent it on gifts for friends and a vacation in the Caribbean. "I wanted to see if I could get away with it," was the only reason he gave us. Quentin and I were both devastated, and Quentin felt humiliated and betrayed, but acted as if he'd expected as much. "You've never had an ounce of ambition," he yelled at Bubbie, who sat in our living room and nodded placidly, which infuriated Quentin and broke my heart. And then, with no warning, six months into his two-year probation, Bubbie left town. Every morning I looked for an account of his capture in the *Journal*, and every evening I watched the local and national news, sure I'd see him in handcuffs. He never called, but every month he sent a cryptic postcard. I kept them in a dresser drawer, occasionally laying them out, arranging them in the order he sent them, rereading them, studying the pictures.

The first one came from Mt. Rushmore and said, "I've been helping a farmer with his wheat harvest." Bubbie'd never been near a farm in his life. Right away I thought of *North by Northwest* and wondered if he'd gotten himself involved with a ring of spies, like in the movie. From Eastport, Maine, he wrote: "I'm a busboy in a busy seafood restaurant." I'd seen a "Frontline" program about heroin smuggling on small fishing boats. And from Alabama: "I'm living in a remote cabin, hunting for my supper." A remote cabin was an ideal place to hide stolen car parts, and "hunting" was surely a euphemism.

I told Quentin that Bubbie could be sending coded messages because he felt guilty and wanted to confess to us, but not to the police, should they ever get their hands on the cards. "Look in the dictionary under 'delusional' and there'll be a picture of you," Quentin told me one blizzardy night, holding the postcards above the trash can. "Face it, darling," he went on. "Our son's a common thug." While he was talking I managed to snatch the postcards out of his hand, knowing in my bones that one day I'd be proven right.

I heard a rustling noise and glanced over at the next cafe table. There sat a fortyish woman wearing a royal blue suit, her dark hair pulled back with a gold barrette. The rims of her glasses were speckled pink and blue. She was reading the *Journal* and sipping hot water with lemon from a teacup, obviously brought from home. She could have a secret life as a madame, I thought. Or a baby seller. Or someone who arranged marriages between poor Taiwanese girls and tyrannical Midwestern dairy farmers. "Excuse me," I said.

She turned toward me. Two front teeth gleamed above her lower lip like pearls in a red velvet case. I remembered how Bubbie, when he was ten years old, used to run around the house shouting, "Kiss me buck tooth! My tonsils itch!"

"Do you work in a dress shop?" I asked her.

"Bennett's Shoes," she said, holding up a slender foot so I could admire her leopardskin pump.

I'd start out by making her guess what I wanted. "Do you go to The Grass Shack? I mean, have you been there recently?"

"Do I know you?" She folded her newspaper in half.

I decided to change tactics—put her on the defensive. "The cook there told me you took the owner's cigarette lighter, a pink one, shaped like a pelican."

"He gave it to me."

Ah-ha, I thought. I said, "There's only one of those lighters in existence. Why do you suppose I found it in my house this morning?"

"Are you implying I put it there?"

"If you didn't, maybe you gave it to someone who did. Or something."

She said, "Why does it matter?"

"The way it was placed, in my fruit bowl," I said. "Somebody snuck in and left it there, like some sort of message. Or warning. I know it sounds nuts." My hard-nosed sleuth persona had shriveled up and died.

The woman stuck out her hand for me to shake. "Jean Coomer," she said. Her front teeth slid all the way out, which was embarrassing, as if her slip was showing.

It was no use. I shook her hand. "Francine Brick."

"I've seen you before," Jean said. "Quad A, right? I used to fill in for a gal at the Bennett's downtown. How many pairs of black shoes do you own, anyway?"

"Twenty-nine," I said, wishing I was exaggerating, cursing once again the smallness of the town. I drained the rest of my mocha, thinking of all the shoes lined up in my closet, shoes I'd bought secretly and snuck into the house, feeling wicked when I casually put them on and paraded in front of Quentin, acting like I'd always owned them.

Jean scooted her chair around till she was facing me. "I named that little pelican Peter," she said. "I use him to light the candles at St. John's. I hid him pretty good, back behind the pulpit, but I guess somebody could've swiped him. And now he's turned up at your house. You live alone?"

I nodded.

"Move in with a friend. A deranged psychopath could be stalking you."

"Is there any other kind of psychopath?"

Jean frowned, as if she were the one being stalked.

"But I like living alone," I said.

"Always been a single gal?"

"Divorced."

"Me too." Jean took a sip of hot water, her upper lip slipping over her teeth. "I don't get men. I just broke up with some guy who thinks he's the King of England."

"My ex-husband idolized Mark Spitz."

Jean said, "There you go," as if we'd just proved something.

"He hung up that ridiculous poster in our bathroom," I went on, "and tried to grow a big mustache. He bragged to everyone that Mark Spitz had gone to IU, just like he had, and they'd both gone to IU Dental School. See, when Quentin was in high school he broke an Arkansas record in the butterfly."

Jean's eyes were wide behind the speckled glasses. "Maybe *Quentin* put the lighter there, you know, to punish you. Make you think you're going crazy."

"I'm already crazy, according to him."

"Do you know any other strange people? I mean, besides Quentin?"

I didn't like how this had turned around—she was the one questioning me. "Just a few weirdos in my pottery class," I told her.

"Weirdos always take those classes," Jean said, not realizing she was including me. "Artiste, eh?"

"Hardly." I was always trying to find something I was

really good at. At IU I'd majored in Home Ec, because spying never seemed like a real career choice. Over the years I'd thought about becoming a journalist, since they are similar to spies, but I was too busy shopping to go back to school.

Jean said, "Any enemies?"

"I worked in Quentin's office for a while, trying to convince people to pay their bills."

"Bingo," said Jean.

"But that was back in the seventies."

"Who hates you?" she said, her voice insisting that someone must.

I laughed nervously. "We had a nasty neighbor who poisoned our dog, but he's in a nursing home. Let's see. I quit going to Book Club. I don't see much of my old friends anymore, but I try to get out and do things, just to keep busy. First my son left, and then when Quentin left I practically went into hiding." I knew I was babbling, but I couldn't remember when I'd last had a conversation with someone.

"Any recent visitors?" Jean said. "Smokers?" She was a better detective than I was.

"Just some women from First Presbyterian," I said. "But they don't smoke."

"You'd never know it if they did."

"My son's mixed up with some bad people." I expected her to ask me more about my son, but instead she said, "Whose isn't?"

She dabbed her mouth with a napkin, leaving a raspberry lipstick smear on her teeth. "Don't let me see your face on the evening news," she warned me, like I'd be personally letting her down if I was murdered. "Here's my vitals." She scribbled her address and phone number on the front page of the newspaper, ripped it off and gave it to me. "I'll discuss this with the priest," she said. "If it's somebody from St. John's, we'll catch the bastard."

"Oh, don't bother, really," I said. I folded the paper and

tucked it into my purse. "Your buck teeth aren't the least bit scary," I added, hoping too late that she wouldn't be offended.

"They make me look distinctive," she said. "Don't you think?"

ST. JOHN'S EPISCOPAL CHURCH

Although there was only a slender thread leading me from the mall to St. John's, I hoped that this was the path my adversary, as I was beginning to think of him, intended me to follow. On the way downtown it started to rain, a hard rain that looked like it might turn to sleet. I caught every red light, and while I was waiting, warming my hands under the vent, inhaling the soggy smell of my Cadillac, I thought about Jean and how nice she'd turned out to be. But perhaps she was only pretending to be nice. Naming the pelican Peter was really too cute. She had given me her name and address, but of course anyone could call herself Jean Coomer. I wondered if I'd underestimated her, thinking of her as a madame or baby seller. Supposing *she* was the deranged psychopath? Why had she immediately brought up stalking, when I was only talking about a cigarette lighter? She might not even be aware that she'd been stalking me. I'd heard on NPR about a woman who had multiple personalities, and the police caught one of her personalities sending hate notes to the other ones. Or supposing she was mixed up in a con game with her "King of England"? Even if she was only a sweet little church lady, I'd been stupid to reveal so much, and I promised myself I wouldn't do it again.

St. John's was a sprawling building with gray siding, modern in a hideous 1960s way. I parked right in front, ran through the cold rain to the side door, and found myself in the sanctuary, which was barnlike and very unimpressive. I stood in the aisle and remembered a wedding I'd attended there a few years ago—the Christmas greenery and candles, the bridesmaids' red velvet dresses, the bride and groom swaying on their feet, and Bubbie, handsome and broad-shouldered in his tuxedo, as best man. Quentin, who shrank from any emotional display, studied the ceiling, but I couldn't take my eyes off Bubbie, who looked so strong and capable and solid. Even if he isn't brilliant, or brimming with self-confidence, I thought, his day is coming. I pictured him in the backyard of a little National home, pushing one of five blond daughters on a swing, a doting wife watching from the kitchen window.

"Have you ever done this kind of thing before?" Quentin asked Bubbie after he'd pled guilty to stealing from the SireShop. "What other crimes have you committed?"

"Just shoplifting, now and then," Bubbie said. "No more than usual."

"Usual? What's usual?" said Quentin, who'd probably never even stolen a paperclip, or at least would never admit to it.

I blurted out, "I went through a shoplifting phase in college. My roommates and I used to steal food from grocery stores, like caviar and champagne, so we could throw extravagant parties." Actually, I'd never done that, but my roommates had. Bubbie smiled gratefully, but Quentin glared at me and said, "Thank you, darling," and I realized that he'd grown as tired of me as he was of Bubbie.

Standing alone in St. John's sanctuary, I blinked back tears, and the altar and stained glass windows blurred together. I couldn't waste time thinking about all this now. I had a mission. I continued down the aisle, toward the altar, but then I remembered that Peter the Pelican wasn't there, he was at my house. If I was going to find out anything, I needed to talk to someone.

There was no secretary in the outer office, so I walked on through, my footsteps muffled by thick red carpeting. In a small back office lined with books, a priest sat behind a walnut desk reading a paperback Western by the light of a sleek desk lamp. As soon as he saw me he slipped the book into a drawer and straightened his priestly collar.

It was the priest who'd performed the wedding ceremony—a young man only a couple of years older than Bubbie. I couldn't think of his name, but years ago, when the boys were in grade school, he'd come to a spookhouse in our basement. At the wedding reception he and Bubbie had chatted for quite a while, which surprised me at the time. But now it made sense. It was a brilliant ploy to involve an actual priest in this game. "I'm Bubbie Brick's mother," I said, but he gave me a blank look, sly devil. "I need help," I said.

"Sit down," he said, not very enthusiastically, pointing to a puffy floral armchair, and I did, slipping out of my jacket.

He looked at his watch, a huge watch with all kinds of dials and knobs on it, a sportsman's watch. He was so fair that his eyebrows and eyelashes were invisible. I tried to remember anything I could about him from the wedding and could only recall him using the word "special" over and over again till I thought I'd scream. How long had he been on the wrong side of the law? A bad priest was a horrible thing, like a baby on crack cocaine.

I didn't want to bring up the lighter right away, like I had with Jean. "Are you a skin diver?" I said, pointing to his watch. "Good weather for it."

"I've got to be somewhere soon," he said. "What seems to be the problem?"

He was trying to get rid of me. I needed an approach, so I did the obvious. I said, "Father, I've done some terrible things."

"Such as?"

"Remember that spookhouse you came to in our basement?"

He shook his head.

I twisted my skirt straight and settled in. "Well," I said, "I set up that spookhouse for the sole purpose of scaring Bubbie. I pulled my turtleneck up over my head and walked around with a pumpkin under my arm saying, 'My head fell off. My head fell off.' Bubbie ran away crying and locked himself in his bedroom. Isn't that terrible?" The priest's expression didn't change. "And another time," I said, "I convinced Bubbie there was an escaped maniac on the loose, lurking about our house, a creature half-moose, half-man, called the Moose Man, with an evil mooing laugh."

"Could you demonstrate?" the priest said.

"Moooooo." I smiled a sick little smile.

"Not too scary," the priest said, and for some reason I felt slighted.

I tried again. "Once I told Bubbie that our neighbor had been married five times and had probably murdered all his wives. The next thing I know, Bubbie is over in the neighbor's yard digging holes with a shovel, looking for bones. Destroyed that man's entire yard."

"Did he find any?"

"Bones? Of course not. That's what I'm telling you. I made it all up."

"You never know." The priest was studying the chrome lamp on his desk. "That lamp was a special present from my wife," he said.

Why had he mentioned a wife? Did he think I was trying to seduce him? Was he paranoid about being taken for a homosexual? Or was "special present" some sort of code? I needed my wits about me with this one. I dug my heels into the carpet, trying to gain control of myself, but something about the priest's face made me want to keep talking. Maybe it was his lack of eyebrows. I couldn't imagine telling these things to anyone else, especially my own minister, an imposing, beetle-browed man, who when asked how he was doing would always bellow, "On-ly ter-rific!"

I went on. "Bubbie's so easy to tease," I said. "Once, when he was in high school, I saw his Mustang parked downtown and I put a note under the windshield wiper that said, 'You'll get yours.' All day long I chuckled to myself, knowing he'd be wondering who could possibly be after him and what he'd done wrong. When I told him I'd written the note, he blew up and said he'd been terrified out of his mind and had spent the day sitting in front of the police station. I kept insisting it was only a joke. I shouldn't have done that. Why did I?"

"Because he's easy to tease?"

"You know what I mean. How could I have done that to my own child?"

"I'm just trying to put things in perspective," the priest said. "But it does seem a bit unkind." He sighed and slid down in his seat. "I just can't decide whether I like that lamp."

I wanted to knock the lamp off his desk. "I was more than unkind," I said. "I was cruel." I had no idea if other parents did these sorts of things—I knew Quentin didn't. I'd probably warped Bubbie's personality while attempting to change it, determined that he would not remain a literal-minded boy who only saw what was right in front of his nose. Quentin had his own method of pushing Bubbie in new directions. He went to all of Bubbie's swim meets, barking out instructions from the bleachers, and was forever reminding Bubbie that, if he got off his butt, he could get a swimming scholarship to IU and become a professional—a dentist, or a doctor or lawyer. But during his junior year, Bubbie quit the team, saying he was tired of getting up at 5 A.M. for practice. After Bubbie stopped swimming, Quentin started swimming again, dragging himself out of bed to do laps at the Y, which always seemed like punishment to me, but I could never be sure who he was punishing.

I could hear the pleading note in my voice even before I addressed the priest. "Don't you think that Bubbie's father and I are responsible for the way he turned out?" I asked him. "Otherwise, the world is just too scary and unpredictable. Too much like an episode of 'Unsolved Mysteries.'"

"Shows like that should be taken off the air. They only encourage unstable minds." The priest rapped his knuckles on the desk. "That lamp just doesn't go in here," he said. "Think I'll return it."

Was he trying to make some connection between "lamp" and "lighter"? I felt panicky, out of breath, and I covered it up by closing my eyes and clasping my hands like I was having a religious swoon. It was then I saw a way to bring up the lighter. "I'd like to light a candle," I said, "to pray for my son."

"We don't do that here," he said. "That's the Catholics."

"Jean Coomer told me she lit candles," I said. "With a little pelican lighter called Peter." I watched his reaction carefully, but he just nodded.

"Jean and Bill Talmidge light candles, but only on Sundays, as part of the church service. I paired them up because they're both single, but I'm afraid they don't even like each other." He scowled at the lamp. "My wife thinks I'm meddling."

"Bill Talmidge," I said. "Isn't he the one who works at Ross Gear?"

"He's a partner in a law firm downtown. I really need to go now." He stood up, reached under his desk, and pulled out a gym bag, and I fought the urge to duck. As I was heading for the door he delivered a canned parting speech. "I hope you settle things with your son. Maybe you need to ask his forgiveness."

"Easier said than done." I paused. "I have no idea how to get in touch with him. Last I heard, he was smuggling exotic birds into the country."

"No kidding." The priest dropped his gym bag on the desk, interested in spite of himself. "He and I both played trumpet in the marching band." He smiled at me, looking for the first time like the boy he was.

"So you do remember us," I said.

"Of course," he said. "Come back anytime you want to talk, Mrs. Brick. Anytime."

BURNS AND BURNS ASSOCIATES

As I drove toward the courthouse square, my windshield wipers flinging themselves uselessly back and forth, I wondered how Bill Talmidge fit into the picture. Maybe the priest was sending me to him as part of some weird scheme to recruit me to their church. Or maybe he was a friend of Bubbie's and he'd been instructed to pull a rabbit out of a hat—a wad of ill-gotten cash to assist me in my old age, which I would, of course, turn down. Or maybe he'd tie me up and throw me in a closet. I was getting smarter as the day wore on, and I decided not to take any chances—I would pretend to be someone else. I stood in a phone booth on Main Street, looked through the phone book, and discovered that there were five law firms downtown. I found Bill Talmidge at the first one I called. I told him I was a reporter for the *Journal*, and that I was asking local people their opinions about the restaurants in town. He actually agreed to be interviewed in half an hour. Elated with my success, I stopped at Walgreens and bought a cheap umbrella and a small notebook, the kind I imagined reporters must carry. As I walked the two blocks to the Jefferson building, the umbrella pulled down on my head like a hat, giggling like a fool, I wondered if I'd come totally unraveled, my mind being already unstable, as the priest had insinuated, but then I decided that I was still sane or I wouldn't even be concerned about it.

Bill Talmidge was a disturbing man. He was in his late fifties, had a rectangular-shaped head, and wore a plaid polyester blazer. There was a wart on the side of his nose, a wart which could've easily been removed. When he shook my hand, I noticed that he wore a signet ring with some sort of symbol etched into the gold—probably a cult symbol. I introduced myself as Linda Smith, a new reporter for the *Journal*. When sitting at his desk, Bill was framed by a big window which looked directly out at the Wabash building, where Quentin's dental office had been. I had a clear view of Quentin's old office, which made me even more nervous, but I managed to sit down with some grace in a wobbly chair facing Bill and ask what he and his family thought about the local restaurants.

"My dear wife is no longer among the living," he said with a faint British accent. "And our children have moved on to greener pastures." He picked up a framed photograph on his desk and showed it to me—a line of dark-haired people standing on the deck of a ship. "The QE2," he said.

It was too much of a coincidence—both the King *and* Queen of England mentioned in one afternoon. But what to do with this information? I glanced around to see if there were any diplomas on the walls, diplomas which might have another name on them besides Bill Talmidge, but there was only a framed poster of the Tower of London. "You're from England?" I said.

"I'm from right here, the benighted village of LayFlat, born and raised." He rubbed his hands together, making a dry rasping sound. "But I travel around Great Britain every summer and immerse myself in her culture, enough to last me till I go again."

I wrote *liar, liar, pants on fire* in my little notebook. "Shall we move on to the restaurants?" I asked in my Linda Smith voice.

Bill gave me detailed descriptions of what he'd ordered where, and how it had tasted, and surprisingly enough, he seemed to like everything. Even if he was making it up, it sounded authoritative, I thought, as I jotted down his answers. Maybe I'd actually write the article and send it to the *Journal*. "Have you tried The Grass Shack?" I asked him.

"Oh yes. Dined there day before yesterday." He gave me his judgments about the place, again all positive, keeping his eyes fixed on mine, which made me feel as if he was complimenting me.

I sat up straight in what I hoped was a professional manner. "And what made you choose The Grass Shack?" I said. "Advertising? Word of mouth?"

"I happened upon one of their novelty cigarette lighters. Well, to be truthful, I stole the lighter from a young lady I was seeing. Who now fancies herself in love with a priest."

Did he mean Jean Coomer, in love with the boy priest? Was the priest in love with her? Where did that leave the priest's omnipresent wife and her ugly lamp? But I couldn't ask any of these questions without giving myself away. I said, "Do you still have it?"

Bill cocked his head, puzzled.

"The lighter, I mean. I'm always curious about successful advertising. It's a real interest of mine." Linda was on a roll.

He folded his arms behind his head, twisting this way and that. "I took it with me to The Grass Shack, because of the address. Believe I left it on the table."

There's my cue, I thought, slipping my arms into my jacket.

"Hold on," Bill said, changing his tone completely. "Perhaps we could meet at the Shack sometime. Discuss advertising at greater length."

I wondered if this invitation was spontaneous, or a pre-planned tactic. Either way, it was probably best to stay in character. I figured that Linda Smith, poor lonely soul, would definitely be tempted, warty nose and all. But she would be coy, at first. "My husband wouldn't like it," I told Bill. "He's a policeman."

"Haven't you ever done anything like this?" he said, as if we were already doing something. "A good-looking woman like yourself?" He flashed me an off-kilter smile, insulting and flattering me at the same time.

"How good-looking am I?" Linda needed such reassurances.

"Oh very," Bill said. "And you seem like such a fun person, too."

The rain began to ping icily against the window, making the room feel cozy, apart from the rest of the world, and I was unnerved to discover that I felt more comfortable being Linda

Smith than I did being myself. I glanced over at Quentin's old windows as if I might catch a glimpse of him standing there between the desks in his white smock, pointing his drill accusingly at me.

Bill cleared his throat. "There's a story behind those windows," he said. "Off the record, of course."

"Of course."

He swiveled to look up at the windows, as if he, too, could see Quentin. "Some dentist used to have his office up there," he said. "After hours he'd parade in front of the window wearing nothing but a Speedo and a bunch of medals around his neck. It was quite a spectacle. The secretaries loved it."

I flailed about for a handhold. "Did he look like Mark Spitz?"

"It was red, white, and blue, the Speedo. There's an insurance agency up there now. All business, those fellows."

I closed my notebook and stood up. "Thanks so much," I snapped.

"Do you have to run off?" Bill looked so surprised that I could tell he had no idea who I really was or what he'd done. "What about that drink?" he said. "When's a good time for you?"

"Right now," I said, and walked out the door.

BACK TO THE GRASS SHACK

Outside it was sleeting, and a thin glaze of ice covered the sidewalk. The umbrella was useless and so were my loafers. I minced back toward the car, holding on to the sides of the limestone buildings, and did a half-assed job of scraping my car windows, my bare hands freezing. I started the car, and although my house was only half a mile from downtown, I drove in the opposite direction, peering out of the foggy hole I'd scraped in the windshield. It was three o'clock, too late for lunch, too early for dinner, but I hoped The Grass Shack was still open. Every muscle in my body felt tense, and it wasn't just the ice. How could I not have recognized that I was living with an exhibitionist? Look in the dictionary under *pervert*! Surely it was a perversion to prance around half-naked, showing off, pretending to be somebody else? And who was he showing off for? A particular legal secretary, or the citizens of Greater Lafayette? It made me sick to picture it, and I wouldn't be picturing it now if there hadn't been a lighter in my fruit bowl this morning. I couldn't believe that someone had put a lighter in my fruit bowl just so I'd find out that my husband was a Mark Spitz impersonator.

When I pulled into The Grass Shack parking lot it stopped sleeting. I noticed that the neon light was off, and the same two cars were parked there, along with a third car, a dark blue Honda.

"Hello!" I bellowed when I stepped inside. "Me again."

A bartender stood behind the ship-shaped bar, his back to me, drying glasses and stacking them in a cupboard. "We're closed," he said. Before he'd even turned around I knew it was Bubbie. He looked nothing like the Bubbie of my "Unsolved Mysteries" fantasy who was sweet-talking the old woman in a bar. That Bubbie had sunken cheeks, a stubbly chin, and hard, glittery eyes. The Bubbie standing before me still had a smooth face, wispy hair, and glasses. My baby. "Hi Mom," he said, stepping out from behind the bar.

I rushed over and gave him a hug, and underneath the smell of smoke and grease I could smell the old Bubbie, a smell like fresh graham crackers. I wiped my eyes and pushed him away.

"Cool sweater," he said, plucking at one of the sunflowers.

"What's the meaning of this?" I said. "What're you doing here?"

He grimaced in his familiar way, pushing his wire-frames up on his nose. "I've been working here a couple weeks."

"Why didn't you call me?" My voice sounded whiny, like a child's. "You planted that lighter just to get even with me. Only this was worse than anything I ever did to you. Sending me on a wild goose chase all over town." I stopped to take a breath.

Bubbie was smiling. "I didn't do it on purpose. Where'd you find it?"

"Right where you left it. In the fruit bowl."

"I was playing with it when I went in, and when I came out I didn't have it, but I didn't have time to go back and look. I just wanted to walk around the house and reminisce." He leaned against the counter behind the bar, and I noticed with dismay that the denim shirt he wore was way too big for him. "I did take a tangelo," he said.

I dropped down on a bar stool. "Fix me a drink," I said.

Bubbie wheeled around and grabbed a glass. "How about a whiskey sour?"

"Where have you been all this time?" I asked him. "What've you been doing?"

His hands, when he poured the whiskey, were trembling. I wondered if he was expecting the police to come bursting through the doors any minute. "Didn't you get my cards?" he said.

"There must've been more going on. Things you weren't telling me."

"Nope." He dropped a plastic hula dancer in my drink and set it in front of me. "Want to try our pu-pu platter?"

I reached over the bar and squeezed his arm. "Honey," I said. "Are you going to jail?"

"Guy who comes in here's a lawyer. He's working out a deal for me."

"Have you done anything illegal anywhere else?"

Bubbie wrapped the bar rag around his hand like a bandage. "Actually," he said, "I haven't been anywhere except Kokomo. Been working at The Grass Shack over there. I got friends to send those postcards for me."

"Kokomo?"

He nodded.

In the silence I heard tinny Polynesian music wafting down from the ceiling.

Bubbie turned and walked through the swinging door into the kitchen. "Pooey!" I heard him yell.

I took a swallow of my drink, and then another. I felt so warm I slipped out of my jacket. In the kitchen I heard Bubbie and another man, probably the horse-faced cook, laughing, probably at me. I set my empty glass down hard on the bar and Bubbie popped back out through the swinging door with a pu-pu platter, which he set down in front of me. The pineapple was already turning brown in the grease, which was pooling up under the skewers. Sweet-smelling steam rose in my face. With Bubbie back in town, no longer in trouble, working at a horrid little restaurant, where did that leave me? I already felt nostalgic for my isolation, for "Unsolved Mysteries," for the exotic postcards from Kokomo.

"Greetings," somebody called from behind me. It was Bill Talmidge, clomping up in rubber boots. He tossed his tweed overcoat over the prow of the bar and sat down on a bar stool beside mine. "Sorry it took me so long." He smiled at me as if we were on a date. "Hoist up a Bass ale, sailor," he said to Bubbie.

I watched Bubbie lift the lid of a cooler, take out a bottle of beer, and pour it into a frosted glass for Bill. Then he made me another whiskey sour, returning the plastic hula dancer to my freshened drink. Her eyes were done in harlot black, but her mouth was a vulnerable little O, like a child playing dress-up who hadn't finished her makeup, like Mark Spitz without a mustache.

"Mind if I indulge?" Bill pointed at the pu-pu platter, and I pushed it over in front of him. He lifted a skewer to his mouth and sucked it clean. "Tasty," he said.

"This is the lawyer I was telling you about, Mom," Bubbie said. "He's helping me with my case."

"Bubbie's your son?"

I couldn't meet Bill's eyes, so I turned to Bubbie. "He

thinks my name is Linda and I'm a newspaper reporter and I'm married to a policeman. I guess I better straighten him out."

Bubbie snorted. "I guess."

"No need," said Bill, holding up his hand. "I knew all along you weren't Linda Smith of the *Journal*. I know everybody down at that sorry rag. I'm just delighted you popped into my office, for whatever reason. My day was shaping up to be another dull one."

"Didn't I seem like a reporter, though?" I asked Bill. "I had a notebook."

"I'm intuiting that your mum is a rather unusual woman," Bill said.

Bubbie raised one eyebrow and stared pointedly at Bill. "How is *Jean* these days?"

"I am sorry to report," Bill said, "that Ms. Coomer and I recently parted company."

"So you're the King of England." I pictured him sitting behind his desk, dipping his pinkie ring in hot wax to seal a letter, a furry purple robe draped over his polyester blazer.

"You know Jean?" Bill asked me.

"We're friends," I said. "In fact, I'm going to see her at Bennett's tomorrow, to buy my thirtieth pair of black shoes."

"No kidding."

"And I know the priest at St. John's," I said. "He's the one who sent me to your office."

"Extraordinary," said Bill. "A priest, mixed up in all this."

"That's exactly what I thought."

Bubbie and Bill were both silent, anticipating my explanation, but I didn't want to give it just yet. I wanted to prolong the moment, prolong the entire day. I stirred my drink with the plastic hula dancer and decided that I would take her home with me. I wondered if she might like Peter the Pelican, seeing as they were nearly the same size, and this thought made me unaccountably happy.

Search and ReScue

CHARLOTTE OPENED a new test booklet to the same old words. Is, dig, bed, hop. Watching her hand move down the page, she scribbled in the ovals with her blue pen, marking each word correct or incorrect. She picked up another booklet and started again. Is, dig, bed, hop.

"How's your father this morning?" Pink asked Charlotte. Pink—her full name was Wanda Pinkerton—sat across the table from Charlotte, but her voice was so soft that at first Charlotte always said, "What? What?" until she got used to listening under, instead of over, the sounds of printers clattering and telephones ringing.

"He's still breathing," Charlotte said, poking an oval a little too hard with her pen. She wished she'd never told Pink about her father, because now Pink asked about him every morning. Is, dig, bed, hop.

Charlotte and Pink were employed by the Standardized Testing Company of Lafayette, Indiana, which, according to its handbook, "compiles and grades tests which measure the skills and knowledge of students from every state in the nation." Charlotte wondered why she and Pink couldn't have been assigned Hawaii's tests, or Alaska's, instead of Oklahoma's. Then she could have imagined that the children, after they'd finished their tests, had gone out to make sand castles beside the ocean, or had ridden home on dog sleds. If there was a duller place than Indiana, Charlotte thought, it must be Oklahoma.

A computer had already tabulated the scores of each booklet through page fifteen, but on page sixteen were four spelling words that all first graders in Oklahoma had to know, and the large wobbly letters, written in pencil, had to be judged by the human eye. Charlotte and Pink made a decision about each word and filled in an oval accordingly, as if they were taking a test themselves.

Charlotte dabbed at the ovals in a slapdash manner, but Pink took pains, shading in the ovals carefully, never a stray mark. Each time she finished five booklets she would select another marker from a row of markers in front of her, placing the most recently used one at the end of the line. Charlotte stuck with one marker until it was a fuzzy nub.

"And how's your mother?" Pink said, still looking at Charlotte expectantly.

"We're all fine," Charlotte said. "Mom stayed home last night so I could go to the symphony. It was mostly Mozart. Did you go?"

Pink shook her head and kept marking.

Of course, Charlotte thought. Ordinary concerts wouldn't interest Pink. Once Pink had talked for nearly half an hour about some museum in Illinois where she'd seen the cargo of an old wrecked riverboat on display. The boat, carrying supplies to the western settlers, had sunk in the 1800s and had only recently been discovered and hauled up from the bottom of the river. The cargo was like new, Pink had said, and she had described it in great detail—ground tobacco in little walnut boxes, ale from Amsterdam, essence of ginger.

Charlotte picked up her mug and took a swallow of tepid coffee, studying Pink over the rim. Pink looked so self-contained, perched there in her tailored blouse and skirt, her arm moving in little jerks down the page. Everything about her was tidy, except for her thick brown hair, streaked with gray, which she pulled back in a sort of bird's nest. Next to Pink, Charlotte felt like a gawky adolescent. Today she was wearing a gauzy turquoise skirt, and when she'd sat down she'd hiked it up over her knees.

Charlotte looked at the column of words on her new page. The letters were scrunched together so closely she couldn't recognize them, but she marked each word correct, something she suspected Pink would never do.

She couldn't decide whether she and Pink liked each other or not. Pink was thirty-seven, more than a decade older than Charlotte. They'd both lived in the town of Lafayette all their lives, but they'd never met until they started work here two weeks ago. That first morning, the manager, who had frosted hair and wore a blazer with gold-tone buttons and matching gold button earrings, ushered them to their table and went off to get their company-policy handbooks. They waited in silence almost a minute before Pink said, in a voice just above a whisper, "I don't understand earrings. But I like yours. Animals, at least, make sense."

Charlotte smiled, not knowing what to say, and fondled one of her polar-bear earrings. It figures, she thought. I get stuck with an oddball.

During the first few days of work, Pink and Charlotte discovered two things—how to pace themselves so that they made their daily quota of 750 booklets, and how to talk while doing it.

Pink explained that her husband, who worked at Eli Lilly making herbicide for soybeans, brought home a steady paycheck, so she didn't have to work full-time. She preferred temp jobs like this one, she said, because she had other interests. Late one afternoon, after they'd made their quota and were sipping fresh cups of coffee, prolonging the grading of their final booklets, Pink confided to Charlotte that she and her husband had been trying to have children for years. The doctors couldn't figure out what was wrong.

"That's terrible," Charlotte had blurted out, before realizing something consoling might have been more appropriate.

Pink shrugged. "Well, yes and no. We've been approved for adoption. We're thinking along the lines of a Korean baby."

Pink's revelation made Charlotte feel she should offer up something about herself in return, so she told Pink that her father had Alzheimer's. He'd started showing symptoms three years ago, the year after he retired from the car dealership. At first, he followed her mother around the house, hovering beside her chair when she sat down to read the newspaper or write letters for the Democratic party. Once, when her mother went into the bathroom to take a bath, she forgot and locked the door, and because the water was running, she didn't hear him jiggling the doorknob. He began ramming the door with his shoulder, trying to break it down. "Marv!" he'd yelled. "Get out here. We've got customers."

Charlotte had finished college by that time, so she'd moved back home to help her mother take care of him. That was two years ago. Now her father was completely bedridden. Charlotte and her mother were like vapors floating around him. Charlotte hadn't touched her piano in months. Whenever she'd started to play, her mother would begin slamming pots and pans or vacuuming the floors, unable to bear the reminder that one day Charlotte would take her music books and leave. Charlotte spent all her free time away from the house—going to movies and concerts, taking long walks. Her friends from high school, including her ex-boyfriend, had all moved away. She had postponed applying to graduate schools, she told Pink. "Mom couldn't manage without me," she'd said.

"I bet she could," Pink had said.

"No she couldn't." Charlotte had clapped her booklet closed. She felt a twinge of frustration, as if she'd had to stop right in the middle of talking about something she hadn't wanted to discuss in the first place. Then there was an awkwardness between them, and Charlotte tried to dispel it by steering the conversation back to inconsequential things—the two old men grading at the next table, different ways to play solitaire, what sort of food she was hungry for. Pink had gone along with this, reminding Charlotte about the spices from the wrecked ship, and then describing her own collection of black pepper tins, even asking Charlotte if she might have any extra pepper tins around her house.

But it seemed that they'd stepped into a carriage with no reins, and the horse kept picking up speed. They'd had an intimate conversation, and their friendship had to go on, gaining momentum, from there.

Charlotte noticed that her pile of finished booklets was nearly twice as high as Pink's, so she slowed down. Is, correct, dig, correct, beb, incorrect, hop, correct. Who in God's name had picked these four words? she wondered. A kid might know lots of other words, but not these four. Her own father had quit school at age fourteen, but he was such a good salesman that he'd been promoted to general manager of the car dealership when Charlotte was still a child. She remembered the only letter he ever wrote her, when she went away to Indiana University. The letter had said he "missed her terably and hoped she was studdying hard," and that he and her mother wanted to come down to visit the next weekend. She'd been so ashamed of all the misspellings that she'd torn the letter up so her roommate wouldn't see it. She never wrote him back, because she didn't want to admit to him, or to herself, how sad she felt about the distance between them, and how relieved she was to be away from both of them. She'd called and told them that she had an important party to go to that weekend, and asked them not to come. She spent the weekend practicing a

Bach two-part invention, over and over, until she couldn't play it at all.

Charlotte took a new booklet and peeked at page sixteen, but the sight of the wildly ticked ovals depressed her. She dug another booklet from the middle of the stack, hoping that this one belonged to a smart child.

At ten o'clock, Pink took a lens paper from the box beside her and began cleaning her wire-frame glasses, something she did every hour. "Charlotte," she said, rubbing at a speck on her lens. "Did you ever have a friend jump off a bridge?" She slipped her glasses back on and looked intently at Charlotte and waited for an answer.

"You mean because they were my friend?" Charlotte said. "Many have wanted to, I'm sure." She tilted her chair back and rocked it, anticipating Pink's next words. This was the way Pink often started conversations. The first thing she said would be jolting, and only indirectly related to her main point. It was a kind of game Charlotte was catching on to, even enjoying. Yesterday, Pink had asked Charlotte if she ever thought about the possibility of aliens living in colonies in the Midwest, masquerading as human beings. Charlotte said no. Then Pink said that her sister believed this and was writing a book on it, and that her sister was in town visiting from LaPorte, and would Charlotte like to have lunch with them at Arby's? Charlotte declined, because she had to go home and feed her father his lunch. She wished she could have gone. Could there be two people in the world as strange as Pink?

Pink was still looking at Charlotte, her expression as serious as ever. "Who do you think goes after people who drown?" she said.

Charlotte was sailing down another page. Is dig bed hop. "I've no idea. Not me."

"I do," Pink said. "I do search and rescue."

Charlotte dropped a finished booklet on her stack and

grabbed a new one. Was Pink, at last, trying to be funny? "That's some hobby," she said.

"I don't consider it a hobby." Pink creased open a booklet. "People call and ask me to do it. I volunteer my services."

How odd, Charlotte thought. I volunteer my services. She gazed down at her booklet, almost expecting to see the phrase flashing on the page.

Pink rapped her knuckles on the table. "I am a certified diver."

"Are you deputized?" Charlotte said. "Are you some kind of cop?"

"Not at all."

"You're pulling my leg, right?"

Pink sniffed and turned her head, fixing her gaze on the far wall of the room, her pen propped in the center of an oval.

"Okay," Charlotte said. "I believe you." She laughed nervously.

After a few seconds Pink began talking, gradually turning her face toward Charlotte. "It started when my neighbor and I took a class in scuba diving at the Y. I had an aptitude for it, she didn't. I went ahead and took more classes by myself. Advanced and so on. Then I learned search and rescue."

"You rescue people who are already dead?"

"They need rescuing too." Under the fluorescent lights, Pink's face was as pale as her white blouse, and her cheeks looked puffy, as if she were holding her breath. Her thin, freckled arms framed her booklet protectively.

Charlotte wondered if those arms could lift a dead body. "What exactly do you do?" she asked Pink.

"I do rivers. They're much more dangerous than lakes or quarries. We go out in teams. I dive with a lifeline and a partner follows me in a boat. It's another world down there. The water is so dirty you can't see your own body, let alone someone else's. It's all done by touch. We have to leave our hands bare."

Charlotte had never heard Pink speak with such eloquence and authority. "You've actually found people?" she said.

Pink tucked a strand of hair behind her ear. "Remember that family who capsized in the Wabash last March?"

Charlotte nodded. It was hard to believe anyone would stick a toe in the Wabash nowadays. Her father used to fish on it years ago, when they could still eat the catfish he caught.

"The parents surfaced early on," Pink said. "They were floating down the river, one following the other." She covered her mouth and coughed once—to make her story more dramatic, Charlotte thought.

"Their children," Pink continued, "didn't come up so easily. The county had grappling hooks out for days and didn't have any luck, so they called me. I dove in and went straight to the baby girl. I knew where to look."

Charlotte stopped grading, her marker poised above the word *hopp*. "You're psychic."

"No, ma'am," Pink said. "I don't believe in the occult. I put myself in the drowned person's place."

This was getting too weird. Charlotte dotted the ovals. All four words incorrect.

Pink said, "I ask myself, where would I go if I was this person, and I was dead? If I could go wherever the water took me? That baby girl was in a hollowed-out spot in a rock. It was like a cradle, just her size."

"Really?" Charlotte saw the manager with the frosted hair appear in the corner of the room. Today she wore a beige suit. She stood by one of the cubicles and seemed to be watching them. They were talking too much and working too little.

"Shhh," Charlotte hissed. She yanked her skirt down over her knees, lowered her head, and tried to concentrate on page sixteen. She thought about a time when she was young, perhaps five years old, when she and her parents were having a Sunday picnic beside the Wabash. Her father had promised to take her fishing later, and while her mother spread out their lunch he twirled her around and around in a way that made her giggle with fear. When her mother called him to help lift the cooler from the car, Charlotte slipped away, through the weeds, to the top of the steep riverbank. She stood and gazed out at the wide, muddy Wabash. Downstream, the water parted around an island. A treasure island. Charlotte teased herself with the notion that she might swim out and hide there, among the sycamore trees that grew along the water's edge, until her parents gave up looking and went home without her.

Just then her father grabbed her from behind and swung her up into his arms. She hung on to him as he carried her away, her chin jouncing on his shoulder. "You were about to slide right down into that river," he said, giving her a squeeze, "and we'd never have seen you again." She had concluded right then that she'd never be able to leave him, because he could read her mind.

Tonight it was her turn to spoonfeed him his dinner—little chunks of roast beef and mushy carrots. She would have to sit close to him and hear his shallow breathing and look at his filmy eyes. Did he know how repulsed she was by him?

Charlotte closed her test booklet. The manager had turned her back to them. She was standing over the copy machine.

Pink's eyes met Charlotte's. "Not to brag," said Pink, "but I found that teenage boy, the one who was trying to swim across the Wabash during the flood. He'd have to have been either real happy or real sad, to try that. I found him crouched under the I-65 bridge abutment. Like he was waiting for me."

The manager picked up a copy she'd made and examined it.

Charlotte whispered, "Ever feel like you get too involved with these people?"

Pink shrugged, coloring an oval. Then she said, "Did you see the news night before last?"

Charlotte nodded, watching the manager stride out of the room with her sheaf of paper.

"That woman," Pink said, "who jumped off Granville Bridge? The one they call Suicide Bridge? The county called and said they might need me to look for her, if they haven't found her by morning."

Charlotte knew Pink must wear scuba gear when she went down, but she could see Pink wearing her white blouse and red skirt and espadrilles, her hair streaming behind her, frog-legging along the bottom of the river, patting the mud, the barbed wire, the rusted barrels. The picture was peaceful, but somehow disturbing. Charlotte gripped the edge of the table, imagining herself on the bridge. "If I ever drown," she said, "I want you to look for me."

Pink tapped her lips with her marker. Charlotte expected her to ask if she was planning on drowning anytime soon, but she said, "Of course." She stood up and stretched. "Well, I'm off to gather honeysuckle," she said, and strolled toward the ladies' room.

Alone at the table, Charlotte forced herself to keep marking. She thought about what Pink had said about putting herself in the drowned person's place. She imagined her father, flat on his back, in his striped pajamas, sliding feet first down the bank and into the river. The current would pull him under and tug him along, in and out of cool pockets of water, toward the island. He would drift up under the roots of a sycamore tree and lodge there, bobbing gently, like a big catfish. She gave up grading and watched the door of the ladies' room, waiting for Pink to step out. She knew it was silly, but she felt like she'd been deserted.

Pink stepped outside the restroom, stopped in front of the bulletin board, and read some notices, then turned and started back. When she'd settled herself at the table, Charlotte said, "So you're going to call in sick tomorrow?"

Pink reached out to the bottle of strawberry-smelling lotion beside her, pumped a dab on her hands, and rubbed them together. "I won't be sick, and I won't lie. If they won't give me time off, I'll quit." She plucked up a booklet and selected a fresh pen from her row.

"Oh no," Charlotte said.

"It's just a job," Pink said.

Charlotte realized she was sweating, even though the place was cold from the air-conditioning. Her tank-top stuck to her back. Is, dig, bed, hop. All correct, but she didn't feel the fleeting pleasure that she usually did. Pink couldn't leave yet. Charlotte hadn't told Pink what her life was really like, how she felt every night when she stepped in through the back door and called out "I'm home!" and her mother, with her purse slung over her shoulder and car keys in her hand, would dash down the hallway, brush past Charlotte and out the door, eager to see her only because it meant that she could leave to attend a meeting—of the Health Board, or the Association of University Women. Sometimes Charlotte wondered if her mother was trying to get away from her, too.

Pink turned a booklet sideways. "My, my," she said, shaking her head.

The manager had returned and was pacing around the room. Charlotte did three more booklets and Pink was still studying the same page, squinting at it from different angles, as if she expected a word to magically transform itself. Finally Charlotte said, "What's the problem?"

"Would you mark this one correct or incorrect?" Pink shoved the booklet toward Charlotte and pointed with her neatly trimmed fingernail. The *d* in bed had a tail, so that it looked like a combination *d* and *g*.

"Correct," Charlotte said.

Pink pulled her booklet back. "I don't know. Correct wouldn't be right, but then neither would incorrect. I can't in good conscience mark either. It's times like these you wish they had a third circle."

"Think of that child in Oklahoma," Charlotte said. She looked around the room for the manager, didn't see her, and

Elizabeth Stuckey-French

122

went on. "Let's say her father cuts her hair and it's always shorter on one side than the other. Maybe he won't let her go to a hairdresser because he's too cheap. Maybe he wants her to look ugly. Maybe he wants to teach her a lesson." She stopped to take a breath. "Or maybe he thinks he does a good job and she looks cute as the dickens."

Pink gave her a peculiar look, smiling and frowning at the same time. She said, "I highly doubt all that," but she marked the word correct.

Charlotte was digging her fingernails into her thigh. Last night, she had stood in the doorway of her father's bedroom, taking it all in. The odor of urine and bleach. The framed photographs on his dresser—one of her dark-haired mother in her wedding dress, and one of herself at a recital, seated at a baby grand piano, her hair tied back in a silly plaid bow. In the bed, her father, in his striped pajamas, lay on his side, the white sheet pulled up to his waist. His knees were beginning to curl up into a fetal position. She couldn't help thinking about how he used to tap-dance in the kitchen. She and her mother would sit at the table, watching him with envy and amazement. "Keep going, Tom, keep going," her mother would say, clapping her hands in time with his feet. "Do the buck and wing, Daddy," Charlotte would shout. It was their favorite dance. He would start in with a great flourish, flinging out his arms, biting his lower lip with concentration, and then his whole body would slip into an easy rhythm, his black shoes clicking and slapping on the linoleum. Before long Charlotte would be dancing too, hopping around, scuffing her feet back and forth, trying to imitate him, but she could never do it the way he did. Seeing him there in bed, lying on his side, rigid as a piece of driftwood, she wanted to run to him. She wanted to grab his shoulders and shake him loose.

Pink tapped her pen on the table, as if she were waiting for Charlotte to say something more about the child in Oklahoma with the bad haircut.

Charlotte looked down and smoothed her turquoise skirt.

It was the color water should be, she thought. "I didn't tell you," she said, "how I get my dad to speak."

"No, you didn't."

"I ask him, the way I did when I was little, 'Granny, does your dog bite?' and he answers, 'No, child, no.' That's all he can say now. Last month he could sing the bass part of three hymns."

Pink reached across the table and took Charlotte's hand. Charlotte's hand was large and damp. Pink's was small and weightless. Both their hands had streaks of blue on them from the markers.

"Have you ever rescued anyone who was still alive?" Charlotte said.

Pink said something.

Charlotte leaned toward her, hoping Pink would repeat it. She couldn't bring herself to say, "What? What?" like she used to.

"If your time's up," Pink said, louder, "you go. It's not the kind of thing to dwell on."

"I'm not dwelling on it." Charlotte snatched her hand back. She stared at the front of a test booklet, blinking until her eyes were dry. Then she said, "What if somebody's time is up and they don't know it?"

Pink was quiet, and Charlotte knew from Pink's frown that she was thinking carefully about what to say. "When I go out to look for that woman tomorrow," Pink said, "you can come along, if you'd like."

Charlotte was disappointed, and realized she'd been expecting Pink to come up with the right solution. "I could never do that," Charlotte said. "What if we found her?"

"Thought I'd offer," Pink said. She paused, then she said, "I've been mulling something over. It might make sense to you, because of your piano playing."

"What might?"

"My reasons for doing search and rescue," Pink said, like she was about to recite a poem. She folded her hands on top of a test booklet. Her face was flushed, and her eyes looked unusually large behind her glasses. "I am trying to keep my mind off my own misfortunes. I am trying to bring some dignity into the world. And I'm trying to give back the merest portion of what's been given me." She bowed her head and flipped open the new test booklet.

The next morning, Charlotte stood on the riverbank and watched Pink and Pink's friend Ray walk down to the river. Pink went first and Ray followed, holding on to the end of a line attached to Pink's harness. In their diving gear, they looked like one alien taking another one for a walk. They waded into the muddy water, sank to their stomachs, and slipped under like they were crawling into a cave.

Pink had explained that Ray would be the pivot diver, kneeling on the river bottom, holding Pink's line while she did a circular search. She would make a wide circle, then a smaller one inside the wide one, then a slightly smaller one, until she met Ray in the center.

Pink began her first circle. Bubbles broke the surface of the water. Charlotte watched intently, expecting something fabulous to erupt from the water—perhaps a green, glittering sea serpent—but there was only an occasional glint from Pink's tank or splash from her flippers. Soon Charlotte became aware of her heart, which was racing along in sharp contrast to Pink's slow movement and the lazy slide of the river.

Pink began her second circle. Charlotte climbed the bank and sat down in the shade of the Granville Bridge, the iron bars crisscrossing above her. A gust of wind whipped the leaves of the sycamore trees, showing their dull undersides. After a while, a log floated by with a crushed Coke can on it. A blue heron came swooping low, legs dangling like broken sticks. A mosquito bit her on the ankle. She scratched the welt. This was probably all there was to it, she thought. Pink wouldn't find anything.

So what was she doing here? She couldn't come up with an answer, except maybe morbid curiosity. She'd had to call in sick and would lose a day's pay. And she'd upset her mother, who'd been left alone to give her father his sponge bath. When Charlotte had opened the door to leave, her mother had called out, instead of good-bye, "Unbelievable!"

What would life be like without her father? Would she go for minutes, even hours, without reminding herself that he was no longer there? She saw herself living in a studio apartment, riding the subway to graduate school. She saw herself crying on a new bed, crying until she couldn't cry anymore. And what of her mother? Her mother would forget to call her. Their letters would be notes—pained and polite. Her mother would dash from meeting to meeting, finding new causes, new friends. She and Charlotte would no longer have anything in common. Charlotte would lose not only her father, she would lose her mother. Even before he got sick, her father had drawn Charlotte and her mother together. They'd joined forces to fill in his missing pieces, to complete him. Now there was almost nothing left of him, but they continued to try to fill the void he'd become, united only by their chores and memories.

There was a loud splash in the river. Pink was swimming close to the center of the river, near a pile of logs and leaves. Charlotte watched her move slowly around the pile, pulling out sticks and logs and setting them loose to float downstream. Then she stopped and hovered in place. Her flippers barely moved, but it seemed to Charlotte as though they were vibrating, like wings. Pink twisted and dove down deeper, struggling, then, slowly, she rose up to the surface. Ray's head popped up out of the water. Charlotte stood up. Pink was cradling something in her arms. She turned in one bulky swing and began to swim, towing the body of the drowned woman. The woman wore blue jeans, but she was naked from the waist up. Her head tilted backward, and her open eyes seemed to be gazing directly at the sun.

There was a black tarp spread out on the bank, and Pink paddled toward it. She came up, still swimming, right beside the tarp. She and Ray lifted the drowned woman onto the tarp.

Pink pulled off her mask and breathing tube. Water streamed down her face. She crouched beside the woman and put the woman's hands at her sides and her sneakered feet together. She closed the woman's eyes with her thumbs.

Ray pulled off his mask, shaking water from his hair. "I'll call in," he said, yanking his flippers off. Barefoot, he ambled up toward a brown van parked under the trees.

Before she knew it, Charlotte was sitting beside Pink and the dead woman. The smell of decay filtered into her nostrils. The woman's breasts were small and pointed—a red lizard was tattooed on her right breast. Her face was greenish and bloated, and her dark hair was matted, full of twigs. "Where, exactly?" Charlotte said.

"Snagged in the brush." Pink tossed her head. "I suspected she'd be there. She worked at Lilly with my husband."

Charlotte imagined this woman at the Lilly plant, wearing goggles and a hard hat, her tattoo well hidden beneath a bra, a T-shirt, and a lab coat. She stood at attention before a huge vat of roiling antibiotics, always pushing the right buttons, pulling just the right levers.

Charlotte noticed that the woman's blue jeans were still stiff and creased—brand new. "Unbelievable," Charlotte said, and then realized she was echoing her mother's parting shot. Charlotte had thought she understood what her mother'd meant, but now she knew she didn't. What, exactly, did her mother think was unbelievable? That Charlotte would just walk out the door? Or that she had even expected Charlotte to stay? Perhaps she meant something else entirely—something personal and secret.

Pink reached over and rolled the sides of the tarp around the woman, covering her, tucking her in, and then sat back down, gazing at the tarp.

Charlotte felt she should sit beside the woman awhile too, that it would be a respectful thing to do. She looked up at Ray, leaning against his van, talking on a car phone, and she thought about how good it would be to walk up the gravel bank in her slippery sandals, the sharp little rocks flipping up between her toes, and climb into her own car, where the hot seat would burn her thighs, and the engine would cough and rattle when she started it up.

Pink smiled at Charlotte. "See you tomorrow," she said. "Thanks for coming."

They stood up and shook hands in one motion.

"Thanks for being you," Charlotte said. It was a phrase she and her mother often said as a joke, but it wasn't funny now.

Pink nodded, accepting the compliment.

A county sheriff's car, red light flashing, came rumbling over the bridge. The car popped off onto the gravel road, but the bridge continued to rattle. Charlotte thought about the woman who'd been shaken loose from those crossbars, who'd jumped from that railing. She wished she was someone from the future, someone who could wave her back.

Leufredus

WHEN I was pregnant with my first child, thirty-one women in Oxford, including my step-daughter Tippy, were due to give birth within three months of each other. Theories abounded as to the cause of this phenomenon—a record-breaking cold winter, some new farm chemical in the drinking water—but nobody knew for sure. We were written up in newspapers all over the country: "Fertile Indiana County to Produce Bumper Crop of Babies," etc. When I first found out I was pregnant I imagined my large self strolling the streets of Oxford and people stopping to inquire how the baby was doing, remarking on my healthy glow, but by the time I began to show, pregnant women were so common nobody gave us a second look. I didn't even get special attention from my husband, because his darling daughter Tippy, who lived with us, was pregnant with twins.

One day in late June, when I was eight months along, I got an invitation in the mail from *People* magazine, asking me to appear in a group photo with all the other pregnant women, a photo to be taken in a cornfield on the edge of town. "Not me," I said to my husband that evening. "They only want to make us look like a bunch of hicks." I was sitting at the kitchen table watching him chop up vegetables from his garden. I'd stopped cooking because it hurt my back to stand for more than a minute.

"We are hicks, hon," he said. He could talk that way because he'd grown up in Indianapolis. When he first saw Oxford he was like an explorer who'd stumbled upon a lost paradise. He'd spent most of his life in apartment complexes and condos, so he'd embraced my life—me and my parents and brothers and the entire town of Oxford, which he called Leave It to Beaverville—with a giddy devotion. At first I'd found his attitude flattering, but we'd been married for three years and reality had yet to sink in. The fire chief runs over dogs on purpose, I told him. The woman who manages the cafe "accidentally" poisoned her invalid mother. My brothers used to make me go door-to-door collecting money for the Mentally Retarded Foundation. "Those things give a small town charm," he said. We lived in a converted chicken hatchery because he thought it was quaint. It was brick, had high ceilings, lots of windows, and wall-to-wall carpet, but we could never get rid of the mice or the smell. I was beginning to suspect I'd married a happy fool.

He stopped dicing carrots and held up the knife. "What about us fathers?" he said. "Why not take a picture of us in front of the hardware store, displaying our tools?" He wore nothing but a pair of plaid shorts which showed off his flat stomach. He was thirty-eight, twelve years older than me, but his graying hair looked like a disguise on a much younger man.

"Hey there, mother-to-be." Tippy loomed in the doorway of the kitchen. Even though she was only five months pregnant, her stomach was bigger than mine.

I waggled my fat fingers at her.

"Greetings, Egg," she said. When they moved to Oxford, Tippy gave her father the nickname Egg because right away he joined the Lion's Club and Friends of the Library and got elected to the Oxford town council. A good egg.

Egg tossed Tippy a tomato. "Hi kiddo," he said.

"Got Rudy and Loretta's medicine chest stocked today," Tippy said. "Everything but a thermometer." She'd known for weeks she was having a girl and a boy, and she'd been calling them by name for just as long. She took a big bite out of the tomato and licked tomato seeds from her lips. "You got yours done, Katie?"

"Haven't had time," I said. "I don't get to hang around the house all day." Egg and Tippy never asked me about my job—interviewing alcoholics for a government research study. Egg once said he really admired me for doing it, but he wasn't interested in unpleasant details, and neither was Tippy, because she didn't want anyone else getting any attention for anything, even for drinking themselves to death.

Egg tossed a rotten broccoli stump into the sink, then cheered like he'd scored a three-pointer. "Beaverville's gonna be a great place for Rudy and Loretta to grow up." He winked at his daughter. Then he smiled politely at me. "And baby X too," he said.

Egg and I still hadn't settled on a name for our baby, because, although we'd been thrilled about it at first, now we hardly ever talked about it. Tippy and her babies had overshadowed us and ours. I knew I should initiate a discussion of baby names, or help with the salad, or wipe the spaghetti sauce off the wall, or fix up the baby's room, which was still a storage closet, but instead I got up and duck-footed into the living room. Tippy dropped her tomato pulp in the trash and followed me, plopping down in my new rocking chair.

I sat cross-legged on the carpet, which smelled like chicken poop, and tried to do yoga, a position I'd seen in one of the books.

"Think I'll call *People* magazine and offer to pose nude," Tippy said. She was always saying and doing things to make her seem more interesting than she really was. One time she and her high school friends got caught walking around Oxford at midnight dressed only in their underwear, wearing dog bowls on their heads. Egg treated Tippy like she was Anne of Green Gables, even though all evidence pointed to the contrary. She'd been living with us the entire time we'd been married, and all the while I'd tried to be tolerant, counting the days till she finished high school and moved out. But on the night of her high school graduation, driving home from the ceremony, Tippy calmly announced her pregnancy. It didn't even occur to Egg to ask who the father was, and when I asked, he shot me a reproachful look. "I can't tell you," Tippy said. "It wouldn't be right," as though the father were the President of the United States instead of one of the shifty-eyed grease monkeys from the high school. She also said she'd decided to keep living with us while she went to Purdue, so we could help each other with childcare. There was no question of her living with her mother, who traveled around the U.S. doing healing-touch therapy. When we got home that night I locked myself in the bathroom and cried in the shower till the water ran cold.

Tippy was rocking vigorously in my rocker. She'd done her hair up in stubby little pigtails and she wore one of her creations—the bottom half of some overalls sewn onto some hacked-up workshirts. She made spending money by sewing old flannel shirts together to make dresses and selling them to rich idiots in West Lafayette. Any day she expected to be discovered and whisked off to Hollywood because of her sense of style, her good looks, and her singing/acting talent. Oblivious, just like her father.

"Your hair looks dumb," I said.

"Good," she said. "That's the effect I wanted." She flipped her braids around like propellers.

In the kitchen, Egg dropped silverware on the table. "Hey, guys, I won't be able to go out Friday night," he called. "Board meeting. You two can celebrate without me."

Friday was Tippy's nineteenth birthday. She leaned toward me and said in a low voice, "Let's skip dinner and go to the Stabilizer. It's dollar-pitcher night." Tippy always told me about the drinking and pot smoking and screwing around she did, thinking, I guess, that she was making me jealous. Or maybe she was trying to be pals. Either way, it was annoying, because I was attempting to be a grownup.

"Now that's a real motherly thing to do," I said, but even as I said it, I thought that it didn't sound half bad. Tippy was more fun when she had a buzz on. "Never drink alcohol when you're pregnant," the books said, so I'd just drink Coke and watch Tippy pickle the twins. Egg would disapprove, and that thought pleased me. Served him right for sticking me with Tippy.

The following morning I left my office in the Purdue Psych building and drove out to Whispering Winds Treatment Center to interview a new research subject. Whispering Winds was housed in a former country club, tucked back on a gravel road, surrounded by oak trees and meadows, but the beauty of the setting could not penetrate the building. I waddled through the first set of doors, checked in with the guard—a precaution against court-ordered patients bolting—stepped up to the desk where a young black woman wearing a spiffy gold blazer sat doodling, and asked for Dub. The light inside was murky and oppressive, like being inside a moldy bottle.

"Where's Dub?" she shouted at a patient shuffling by in his bathrobe.

"Ain't seen him. Whoa," he said, taking note of my pregnant state.

I stepped out of his way. Although I tried not to let on, the patients spooked me—looking as if they'd just risen up from hell and would slide back down first chance they got. Most probands, as we called them, had been in treatment at least ten times. At first I was mesmerized by their tragic stories about car accidents, vicious mothers, club-wielding boyfriends, wrist slittings, lost jobs and lost houses and lost children and on and on, until at last they began to sound like one big collective wail of self-pity and despair. I'd majored in psychology because I thought it would expose me to fascinating pathologies while at the same time reassuring me that I was normal, sort of like an inoculation, and I also had the vague hope that my normalcy might somehow rub off and heal them, but of course neither of these things occurred. I kept at it because it was my first real job and I didn't know what else I wanted to do. My fellow interviewers performed their jobs like efficient machines, but the misery emitted by our clients seemed to soak into my pores, weighing me down, and pregnancy only made it worse.

Dub sat waiting for me in a group therapy room. His hair, on the crown of his head, stuck up like a mitten. He was missing his left arm below the elbow, and a dirty shirt sleeve flapped over the stump. Except for the stump, he looked like most of the people I interviewed. "I'm Katie," I said.

"And I'm a sorry son of a bitch." He thrust out his hand for me to shake. His handshake was firm and confident, which took me by surprise. I sat down across from him, set up my tape recorder, and explained the confidentiality bit, his payment of fifty dollars, that I was going to ask him questions not only about drinking but also about other things related to drinking, and finally, that we might want a sample of his blood. He nodded when a response was called for, a half-smile never leaving his face. I had a hard time not smiling too.

When I started the interview I discovered that Dub wasn't a typical proband at all. He had a master's degree in philosophy from Berkeley. "Ethics," he said. "Can you believe it? I'm a sorry son of a bitch."

"No you're not," I heard myself say, and then, red-faced, I went on to the next question, reminding myself to erase that part of the tape. I'd once gotten in trouble because my boss, Dr. Schmidt, was listening to a tape of an interview I'd done. When the subject said he'd never smoked pot, I said, "Wow, really?"

It took Dub forever to answer the questions, which would have been impossible for a clear-headed straight-arrow to answer, let alone someone who'd lived for years in an alcoholic fog, questions like "Have you ever drunk more than you intended? How many times?" Subjects usually caught on in a hurry that they were merely supposed to guess, but not Dub. "Don't think too much," I told him cheerfully. But still he sat there, twisting up his face, trying to come up with the correct answer, as if he was doing it for my sake. I found myself staring at the posters on the walls, posters made by patients for thera-peutic reasons—cut-out pictures and letters from magazines that said ambiguous things like "Love is a four-letter word." I kept expecting Dub to tell me how he'd lost his arm, but he never mentioned it.

Finally, halfway through the manic-depressive section, after four trips to the bathroom for me and four cigarette breaks for him, Dub's diligence got to me. Although I knew Dr. Schmidt would not be pleased, I reached over and punched off my tape recorder. "Perhaps we'll continue this at a later date," I said, gathering up my materials officiously. I told myself that even someone holding a gun to my head could not make me ask Dub another interview question. As if relieved by this decision, my baby began to roll, and I stifled an impulse to watch.

Dub pointed at my belly and said, "That's one lucky kid."

Tears welled in my eyes, and I didn't know if they were tears of frustration or gratitude. "You'll get your check next week," I said, blinking, telling myself it was probably just my hormones.

On Friday night, Tippy and I drove fifteen miles into West Lafayette to go to the Stabilizer. I'd hung out there in college, and Tippy'd been sneaking in on a fake ID since she was sixteen. The place was nearly empty—only a few booths were occupied by morose students, and the long trestle tables in the middle were empty. The bartender, leaning on the bar, looked half asleep. Then I saw Dub, sitting alone in a booth, a pitcher of beer and a clean glass in front of him. I'd never run into one of my research subjects out in public before, let alone in a bar. I knew I shouldn't speak to him, but I couldn't help it. I walked over and stuck my bulk in his line of vision. "Off the wagon already?" I said.

"I'm a sorry son of a bitch," he said again, but it didn't sound the same. He wore an Oxford-cloth shirt pinned up neatly over what was left of his arm. He tossed his shiny blond mane back from his forehead. "Two pregnant women come into a bar," he said. "Must be the DTs." When I didn't laugh he said, "Don't worry, I won't drink more than I intend to."

"It's not like I care," I said. "I just collect data."

He turned to Tippy. "Nice outfit," he said. "What is that? A bunch of shirts sewn together?" He bit his lower lip boyishly.

Before I could stop her, Tippy slid down into the booth beside him. I hulked over them disapprovingly for a minute, and then I squeezed into the opposite side of the booth, watching them drink, listening to him impress Tippy by describing his travels around the world and the various philosophies he'd held. It was hard not to fall under Dub's spell. Nobody from Oxford ever went anywhere or changed philosophies. I lived on campus while going to Purdue, but, although I constantly complained about Oxford, I never considered not moving back. Countless times I'd drunk myself stupid in the Stabilizer, flirting desperately with frat boys, sometimes hooking one for a month or two. After graduation, though, the frat boys went off to Chicago or Minneapolis, and I met Egg in the library parking lot when he volunteered to help jump-start my car. He didn't tell me about Tippy until our fourth date, and he never told me he'd always had sole custody of her and felt so guilty about the divorce and her lack of a mother that he could never deny her anything or discipline her at all. And now look at the result, I thought, watching Tippy lean against Dub, pat his shoulder, giggle at his jokes. I'm her stepmother, I thought. I should drag her away by the hair.

"I used to hang out in an ashram in Santa Clara," Dub was saying. "I was super-religious, had my own temple. Ever heard of Leufredus?"

Tippy said, "Who?"

"A French monk. Eighth century. Patron saint invoked against flies. The flies were bothering old Leufredus one day while he was praying, and *zap*! They never darkened his door again." Dub shook his head as if he felt sorry for the flies. "A woman called him bald and he caused all *her* hair to fall out. A thief slandered him, and he and his family lost their teeth."

"Some saint," I muttered.

"Hey," Tippy said, scolding me. "Saints don't have to be nice, just intense."

"Anyway," Dub went on, "when I was living in California, I read up on saints, and I decided why not be one. It was a lucrative deal. Never had to work a day. I called myself Leufredus, sat on some pillows in my log cabin, and people came to see me and give me money. I'd promise to get rid of something bothersome in their lives, like houseflies."

"Or teeth," I said, trying to be funny, but they both just looked at me as if they'd forgotten I was there.

"Dub's a bad hat," I told Tippy on the way home that night. We were driving down a two-lane road, the windows open, and the air smelled like rotten bananas—fumes from the Eli Lilly plant. I was about to break every confidentiality law ever written, but I took pleasure in knowing more about Dub than Tippy did. "He's taken every drug known to man," I said. "Couldn't even count his sexual partners."

Tippy, spread-legged beside me in the front seat, just snickered. "I'm meeting him tomorrow night. Pregnant women turn him on."

"But he's a one-armed al-co-hol-ic," I said loudly. I'd had a couple of beers myself. "Besides," I said, "he's *my* alcoholic. I found him first."

She shrugged. "I guess he likes me better."

"What would Egg think?" I said, but she knew I'd never tell him, because I couldn't bear to see his innocence destroyed. And it was useless to appeal to Tippy's sense of right and wrong. She played Joni Mitchell songs on her guitar and told her friends she'd written them, figuring the 1960s were too long ago for anyone to remember.

"Why'd you marry Egg?" Tippy said. "He's so boring." She was drunker than I was. "God bless Egg." She burst into tears. She was acting like Vera in *Auntie Mame*, the role she'd had in her senior musical. Nobody had the heart to tell Tippy she had a mediocre voice, not even the director. Even the audience clapped wildly after she did a number, impressed by her sheer gall. For my high school musical I'd played cello in the pit orchestra.

A great horned owl swooped out of a cornfield, glared at us through the windshield, and then disappeared into another dark cornfield across the road. "If you sleep with Dub," I said, stepping on the gas again, "don't tell me a thing about it."

A week later, when Egg was out at a Methodist Men's Group meeting, Tippy and I sat across from each other at the kitchen table, hunched over our own games of solitaire. I had three aces up, and she didn't have any, but she looked smug, the way she'd been looking since she met Dub. I finally blurted out, "So what was it like?" My skin was stretched so tightly over my stomach that it prickled. Egg and I had stopped having sex when it became like gymnastics and we laughed ourselves out of the mood, but lately I found myself wanting to do it more than ever. The books never mentioned this.

"The things he can do with that stump," Tippy said, pushing my aces aside to make room for one of hers. "I'd give anything to wake up next to him every morning."

I studied my cards again, looking for a play, even though I knew there wasn't one. I'd never had to ask her for details before. "What exactly did he do with the stump?"

"All kinds of things." She fingered through the cards in her hand, pulled out a two of diamonds, and slapped it on the ace.

"Come on," I said.

"Let's just say I'd love to wrap myself around that stump again." She glanced up at me. "You're pouting, Ma."

"I'm fine."

"I've got a plan," Tippy said, snapping down cards on her aces with a flourish. "Dub and the babies and I will go down South. We'll live on a plantation and wrap our heads in rags."

"The rag part sounds feasible." I scooped up my cards, tapped them into a pack, and began shuffling again. "I'm going out to Whispering Winds tomorrow," I said. "Maybe I'll find you a new boyfriend."

"Tell Dub to call me," she said. "If he's there."

"Really?"

She studied her stomach, her face thoughtful. "I feel like Rudy and Loretta are part Dub's now," she said. "They could both be missing an arm. He might have marked them with his stump." She glanced back up at me. "What are you wearing to the *People* magazine picture?"

"A sheet. If I go."

"I ordered a new dress from Mamadear," she said. "Black satin. Maybe I'll get some commercials out of it."

My last proband at Whispering Winds was a crack addict with a long greasy ponytail who couldn't sit still. He paced around the room, spitting out answers to my questions. "How many times have you smoked marijuana?"

"Two hundred and three," he said, not even pretending to think about it. He kept going off on tangents about how he was a trained sous-chef and how his son, now in prison for a drive-by, had raped his daughter, and he kept tearing strips of tape off a dispenser, rolling them into balls and flicking them across the room like boogers. We completed what was usually a four-hour interview in six hours, and I felt like I'd been battered against a brick wall by a fire hose.

On my way out to the car I saw Dub sitting in the courtyard, wearing a white T-shirt and khaki shorts, sunning himself and smoking a cigarette. The fact that he was missing part of one arm seemed like an optical illusion. He looked so good I wondered if he was back in treatment again or just visiting. I walked over and stood beside him. "Dub," I said, and it came out sounding like "duh."

"Oh hi, doll." He squinted up at me. "How's your stepdaughter? Great girl. Too good for me. But who isn't?" He smiled ruefully at his cigarette. "At least they let me sit out here. I go along with the program, even though it never takes. Have a seat."

I sank down in a webbed lawn chair in the shade of an oak tree. A breeze cooled my forehead. I felt relieved, as if now all was right with the world.

"Beautiful day, huh?" Dub said. He pointed to a meadow which used to be the golf course. "Saw thirteen ostriches out there last night," he said. "It was mystical."

"There's an ostrich farm next door," I said, hating the sound of my practical voice.

Dub just smiled. A cardinal sang from the oak tree. There were wildflowers in the meadow—blue chicory and pink asters. It was mystical. I didn't want to go back to the office. I tried to gaze out at the meadow, but found myself watching Dub instead.

"Would you like to know," he said, "how I lost my arm?"

"I guess so." It was strange to be talking to Dub like a person instead of a research subject. It felt natural and wrong at the same time.

Dub took a drag of his cigarette. "Back when I was living in that ashram, being Leufredus, I was a drunk, just like now. Only I convinced myself I had a higher calling. Every once in a while I'd get really stoned and drunk and tell my friends to hold me down and chop an inch off my arm."

I looked down at my own arm, pale but substantial. "Why?"

"To prove I was holy," Dub said. "That's how I convinced people I was a saint. It worked so well I didn't mind the pain." He stroked his stump with his hand. "But one morning I sort of saw the light. After a six-day binge."

"That's crazy," I said.

"It is on the sick side," Dub agreed.

I wondered why I wasn't more repulsed by his story. For some reason it only added to his appeal.

Dub must've read my expression. "You look sweet." He bit his lower lip. "Hope you don't mind my saying so."

"Sweet?" I said, remembering what Tippy'd said about pregnant women turning him on. I wished I'd worn my maternity sundress instead of the denim jumper. Wishing this made me nervous. "So have you seen Tippy lately?" I said.

"Not since that one night," he said.

I kicked my briefcase over in front of my chair and propped my swollen sandaled feet up on it. Dub looked down at my briefcase and must've remembered that I was there on business. "What can I do you for? Should I chop off my other arm for the U.S. Government?"

"Just wanted to say hi." I swung my feet back onto the ground.

"Wait." Dub pulled my chair closer to his and placed his bare stump on my stomach. The stump was pure white. Both baby and I held still.

"It's a boy," Dub whispered. "Sleeping peacefully."

"Good," I said. I couldn't bear the thought of my baby being unhappy or afraid or hurt for even a second. Suppose my baby turned out to be a proband? "Future Probands of America," my coworkers and I called the children we interviewed. "What about after he's born?" I said. "Will he still be happy?"

"Sometimes," Dub said, nodding. "He'll love canoeing, I can promise you that." He drew his stump back. His eyes were the color of chestnuts. "I have to tell you," he said. "I'm very attracted to you. I felt it right away, the day you first interviewed me, when I first saw you fiddling with your little tape recorder, when you first started in with your spiel about locked cabinets and limited access."

My face flushed, and then the rest of me. "I think Tippy's in love with you," I said.

Dub leaned forward, so close I could see the freckles on his nose. Even his sweat smelled good. "Now, what's this?" he said, and he looked so much like a regular person, a person who could live a good life, that I wanted to hug him.

"Promise you'll stop drinking forever," I said, knowing it was the absolute wrong thing to say.

He reached for my hand, like for some reason he had to comfort me, but I pulled away. I didn't want comfort from Dub. I didn't know what I wanted. "Tippy told me she wants to wake up with you every morning," I said. "She thinks of the babies as part yours."

"Really?" He didn't look surprised as much as he did happy. He sat for a while, grinning off into space, and then he slapped his thigh. "This is just what I need to straighten my ass out." He jumped out of his chair, bent over, and kissed me on the cheek. "Thank you," he said. "Bless you."

I said, "Thank *you*, Leufredus."

"I'll be right back." He handed me his burning cigarette, turned, and ran into the treatment center. The screen door slapped closed behind him. "I'm going to be a daddy!" I heard him yell. "It's twins!"

Sunlight was eating up my shade, but still I sat there. All the books claimed that pregnancy was a serene, introspective time, so why was I feeling the need to consort with an alcoholic? I might not be an alcoholic, I thought, but there is definitely something wrong with me. Get up and go, I told myself, but I sat there, flicking ashes off Dub's cigarette, sniffing secondhand smoke, waiting for him to return.

When he did, the cigarette had burned out and he had a strangely earnest look on his face. "I've got to go see Tippy," he said, shifting from one leg to the other.

"Call her up." I was sitting in full sunlight, sweating. I wasn't sure what I'd set in motion, but there didn't seem to be a way to stop it.

He sat down beside me, radiating energy. "I already called her," he said. "Now I've got to see her." He lowered his voice. "I'm court-ordered this time. Thirty days. I've only done five."

His insistence seemed all out of whack. "Can't she come see you?" I said.

He shook his head. "Not in here. Not like this," he said.

I reached over and touched his stump, thrilled by my audacity. The skin was soft and thin, but underneath his arm was muscular and pulsing. I couldn't see any veins, but they had to be there, somewhere. "Tell them I'm taking you to the lab for a blood draw," I said. "I'll bring you back in an hour."

"I won't come back," he said. "I don't need this idiot box."

"That's true," I said. "It doesn't seem to be helping."

Dub said, "If you spring me, you'll be cooking your goose. They'll never let you in here again."

"Wouldn't that be a shame," I said. I felt like I'd taken some sort of drug, a drug that Dub and his kind were most likely very familiar with, a drug that convinced me that I could, and should, do whatever I wanted to do. "Let's go," I told him.

Dub asked me to take him straight to his apartment. He stared out the window of my university car, cradling his stump and bumping his knees together, and only spoke to give me directions. By then I felt like I was tripping. As I turned onto the bypass, the Escort felt as if it were plotting to bolt out from under me. Everything was hyper-real—Dub's hairy knee, a child in a parking lot tossing a blue ball. The movie theater looked like a garish Oriental temple. When I pulled up in front of Valleyview Villas, Dub unfolded himself from the car, said, " 'Bye now," like I was nothing more than a taxi driver, and disappeared between two brick buildings. I sat there for a moment, wondering for the first time if his sudden interest in Tippy was nothing more than his desire for a drink. Either way, I had to admit that I'd enjoyed our ruse more than I'd enjoyed anything in a long time. Did that make me as mentally ill as he was? I drove away, slowly coming down from the Dub drug. It was no fun being bad alone.

By the time I got home the scenery had flattened out to normal and I was left with a queasy aftertaste of guilt. I knocked on the door of Tippy's room. She was sitting at her sewing machine, pedal down like she was racing a sports car. A little girl's dress with a plaid skirt was under the needle. Tippy herself wore a dress of different plaids. Her hair was up in hot rollers.

"Going out?" I asked over the roar of the sewing machine. I sat down on the trunk at the foot of her bed. I didn't want to get comfortable. I had my speech all prepared. I'd only told Dub what she'd told me. Even though I knew she hadn't meant him to hear a word of it.

She wouldn't look at me. "Dub's coming by. We're heading out to the East Coast. Vermont, maybe."

She didn't sound very happy about it. I felt a stab of jealousy, which I covered over with a stern voice. "You won't have much of a future," I told her, "if you start out like this." My finger traced the decoupage Smokey the Bear on the trunk—a leftover from Tippy's cabin-in-the-woods decorator phase.

"Better than staying in Oxford." Tippy flipped up the needle and whisked the dress out of the machine. "The thing is," she said, and turned toward me. Her eyes were puffy. "Dub wasn't really good in bed—he passed out on me. I just said all that to get your goat. But now I'm stuck. He's so excited about being a father."

"That doesn't make any sense," I said, but somehow, in our little world, it did. I shifted uncomfortably on the edge of the trunk, feeling like the weight of my belly was going to pull me onto the floor. I tried for a mature response. "You can make it on your own. You don't need Dub."

"You do. And you can't have him."

I took a deep breath, but it didn't help. "Dub didn't even remember your name," I said. "When I saw him today." He hadn't remembered my name either, but I didn't mention that. There was a horrible silence. No one talked to the great Tippy like this. The words kept coming. "He touched me with his stump," I said. "He predicted that my baby will lead a happy life."

Tippy's face crumpled with disgust. "You look like Patty Duke, going around in those ugly clothes. Why don't you live your own life for once?" I could tell she'd been wanting to say those things to me for a long time. Then she sighed as if she couldn't be bothered with me anymore. She held out the plaid dress. "Here's a going-away present for your baby," she said. "I've been working on it all day. It has a matching hat."

The dress had a blue-and-green plaid skirt sewn onto a little white onesie with blue satin trim. "Thank you," I said, holding it up to my cheek. I knew that she hadn't been planning to give the dress to me, and I knew my baby was a boy, but for some reason that made me treasure it even more. I'd wanted to apologize to Tippy, but it seemed she was the one apologizing to me, not just for going off with Dub, but for leaving me here with Egg.

When Egg came home from playing basketball, I was propped up in my rocking chair with a box of chocolates. He collapsed on the futon couch, working his sneakers off without untying them. He was all wound up about a *Chicago Tribune* reporter lurking around Main Street. "He interviewed me," Egg said. "It was fun."

"Why you?" I popped another chocolate into my mouth. "Limit your intake of caffeine," all the books said.

"They're thinking maybe something's buried under our house," Egg said. "From when it used to be a chicken hatchery. Some kind of growth hormone leaking into the soil."

"She's gone," I said.

"Who?"

"Your daughter," I said. "She ran off with a proband." I expected Egg to spring up and do something, but when he didn't, I kept talking. "I helped him escape from the treatment center today. A hardcore alcoholic, but a nice guy. Somebody I sort of had a crush on." I popped another chocolate into my mouth. "Anyway, I'd introduced him to Tippy a while back and they fell madly in love and now they've run off to Vermont, and it's my fault." I had no idea what Egg's reaction would be, because I'd never been so honest with him before.

He lay there, staring at the ceiling, his profile lit up by the floor lamp, until I wondered if he'd heard me. Finally he sat up and rubbed his head till his hair stood on end. His cheerful mask was gone, and for the first time since I'd known him, he looked his age. "Where in Vermont?" he said.

"You have another chance, with our baby," I said. "A fresh start." I handed him my box of chocolates, but he pushed them aside.

"I've got to go find her."

"She didn't know for sure where they were going." The

hair on my arms bristled, even though the room was warm. "She's an adult," I said. "Leave her be."

"This is exactly what you wanted to happen." His eyes hardened. He saw this as a contest between me and Tippy, and in any kind of contest, for him, Tippy would always win, even if her prize was dubious.

"It's not exactly what I wanted," I said, wondering what that would have been.

But Egg was already in our bedroom, packing a suitcase.

On the evening of the *People* magazine picture, I got dressed up in my new Laura Ashley dress, made for very large nonpregnant women, and walked out to the cornfield. The humidity was so high I felt slick all over. I passed the farm supply store and the old guys who were always sitting at the counter gave me a wave. Egg had been gone for over a week. He'd called twice and sent postcards from all over Vermont, promising to come back for the baby's birth, but I wasn't holding my breath.

"I quit my job," I told him one night when he called. "I told Dr. Schmidt that Dub jumped out of my car at a stoplight, so he didn't fire me, like I hoped he would."

"What are you going to do?" Egg said. "Be a checker at the Jack and Jill?"

"I'm going to be a mother."

From all over Oxford, by foot and by pickup truck, pregnant women were converging on the cornfield. There was the new woman in town whose husband was in management at Purina Chow, the sixteen-year-old girl with terrible blue eyes, the Japanese woman, two teachers from the high school, and of course, Marcia Tolliver in her army uniform. *People* magazine people were rushing here and there, waving clipboards. The photographer, a tall, thin woman who smoked cigarillos and wore little red sunglasses, ordered all thirty-one of us to stand in a line between two rows of corn, up on a rise, turned sideways to expose our bellies. I looked out at the cornfields unfurling all the way to the horizon, at the wispy clouds hanging in the pale sky like afterthoughts. Even with my bulk I felt weightless, like I could drift off at any second and disappear. It was a pleasant sensation, and I could experience it anytime, I realized, if I'd only come up and stand on this hill. I knew I should be unhappy, having no gainful employment and no husband, but I couldn't find it in me.

My baby pushed up against my ribs and I massaged him through my skin, kneading his tiny limbs with my fingertips, and for some reason I thought about Dub cutting off his own arm, inch by inch. "I know why all these women got pregnant," I told Marcia Tolliver, who was standing next to me. "We all decided we're going to add on to ourselves, by having a baby, and make ourselves holy that way."

"I didn't decide any such thing," Marcia said, stepping back. "Anyway, that doesn't explain why we all got knocked up at once."

"Maybe it's a miracle," I said. "I'm going to name my baby Leufredus."

"That's nice," she said, and turned her back on me.

I never thought I'd miss Tippy, but right then, I did. I could just hear her saying, in a high nasal voice, "Now little Louie, how many times do I have to tell you not to play with that hacksaw?"

The photographer snapped pictures from down below, looking up at us. "Say 'whiskey,' Mommies," she said, but I was already smiling.

Professor Claims
He Found Formula
for Ancient Steel

WE WERE eating lunch one day, waiting for my father to come home from work, when my mother revealed her supernatural abilities to me. I was surprised, of course, to learn that she was a sorceress, but I was even more surprised that she'd managed to conceal it from me, her own daughter, for the entire eleven years of my life. And I'd never imagined I could be guided into a trance by my mother, she of the sarcastic remarks and white ankle socks. But on that oppressively hot afternoon, while wasps buzzed at the window screen and the humidity curled the covers of our paperback mysteries inside out, I sank like an anvil into my mother's spell. I fell easily, without question, because her spell centered around my father, like everything else in our household.

That summer, my father was gone a lot. Weekday mornings he worked in his lab at the university, and in the afternoons he taught a materials science class. I know that doesn't sound like much time away, but Mother and I were used to hearing him up in his study, tapping away at his typewriter, so the silence made us uneasy. I felt, and maybe she did too, that at any moment she and I could skip over into a new groove, like the needle skipped on my *Beloved Fairy Tales* record from "The Snow Queen" to "The Ugly Duckling." Then, like poor Gerta and Kay, nobody would hear from us again.

Ordinarily, when my father was away, Mother and I pretended not to notice. I climbed trees, she weeded her vegetable garden, and during lunch we read. But on that particular day, the day of my mother's magic, we gave up on pretense. When my father got home, we were to leave on vacation—two whole weeks in a log cabin on Eagle's Nest Lake. We'd never been to the north woods before, but Aunt Minnie, my mother's sister, had invited us, and we hoped it would be paradise. Our collie, Toopea, was in the kennel, the mail and newspaper had been stopped, and our suitcases were packed and lined up on the front porch.

The oak tree beside our house kept the kitchen dim and cool, and the sun glimmering through its leaves made a mottled pattern on the green linoleum floor, which looked like the surface of a deep, inviting lake. I munched my tuna sandwich, pretending it was fresh fish caught by my father, who'd turned overnight into an expert fisherman. I saw him standing on a dock, his shoulders thrown back, his prematurely white hair slicked back from his boyish face. He was tanned and grinning and holding up an enormous silvery fish.

Mother, sitting across from me at the kitchen table, shut her latest Agatha Christie with a hiss of disgust. "D-u-l-l," she said. She took a pickle from her plate and dropped it on mine.

"I won't eat that," I said. "You touched it."

"We'll be on our way to Minnesota in thirteen-point-five minutes," Mother said. She brushed a swatch of frizzy brown hair out of her eyes, and it fell right back down again. Her forelock, Daddy called it.

"How do you know?"

"He gave them a test," she said, "so he had to stay the whole hour. His class ends at one-thirty. He'll check his office and start home at one-thirty-seven."

"He won't check his office today," I said. "He'll be in too much of a hurry." I added another spoonful of sugar to my iced tea. This was the most we'd spoken to each other the whole morning.

Mother glanced behind her at the Swiss clock with a scene of the Alps on its face—a gaudy, expensive clock my father had bought her on their honeymoon. "Right this second," she said, "at one thirty-two P.M. Central Standard Time, your father, Allen O. Method, is in his office, 442 Papajohn Hall, Indiana State University. He's stuffing things into that dog-chewn briefcase of his."

I could see him in his office, wearing his tan poplin suit and crisp white shirt. On his desk were the green blotter, part of a desk set I'd given him for Christmas, and a chipped teacup Mother'd given him to hold paperclips. He pulled a heavy book called *Blade and Materials Characterization* from the varnished bookshelves above his desk, bookshelves I'd watched him make and install himself. He opened his briefcase and the book disappeared inside.

Mother said, "He leaves the student exams on his desk. Doesn't want to grade papers on vacation, so he forgets them, as you say, 'accidentally on purpose.' "

"Daddy wouldn't forget on purpose."

"He would, and he does." She bit off half a carrot stick.

I frowned in order to hide my delight—my delight at her perceptiveness, her definite tone, the intensity of her focus. Normally, communication between us was hazy and halfhearted. Mother and I saved up all of our energy for my father. At some point, in one of the unspoken agreements families make, my mother and I had started pretending my father was a primitive but powerful god who'd been inexplicably left in our care. I did my part by defending him against the forces seeking to belittle him. I went with him to Sears on Saturday mornings and trailed him as he moved down the aisles in his paint-spattered jeans and baseball hat, fingering the plastic packages of nails, occasionally shaking one as if it were holding out on him. Don't confuse him, I silently pleaded with the nails. Don't surprise him, I entreated the wrenches. If something did trip him up, if there were, say, too many different types of paint thinner to choose from, or if the pricing rationale was unclear, my father might engage the teenage clerk in a discussion which could escalate into an argument, ending with my father dropping the can of paint thinner on the counter and marching out of the store. "Idiot kid," he'd mutter, and I was afraid people passing us would think he meant me. In the car, on the way home, I could feel my father's silent anger, so I talked. "Can you frame my poster today? Of the race horse? Marcia just sticks hers up with putty and they don't look near as good as mine." I kept on till he finally looked down at me and smiled. "Let's swing by Dairy Queen, Dilly Bar," he might say, and then I could breathe again.

My mother took a different approach. She protected my father from inflated expectations. He wasn't a professor of metallurgy, he was a "glorified blacksmith." Indiana State wasn't a university, it was a "high school with ashtrays."

Earlier in the summer, one evening after dinner, my father tapped his ice cream dish with his knife, interrupting a conversation my mother and I were having about which one of us Toopea liked better. "Damascus steel," he announced, "is the Holy Grail of metallurgy. Before Christ it was used to make swords of the highest quality. The formula has been lost for hundreds of years, and metallurgists have been trying to duplicate it, but with zippo luck. I intend to have a Damascus steel sword by Labor Day."

"You will," I said.

"We're still going to Minnesota," my mother said.

My father continued. "Legend has it that the Turkish artisans who made Damascus steel tempered their blades by dipping them in the urine of red-haired boys." He tapped the flat of his knife blade on my wrist. "Perhaps I should try that."

I studied a scab on my knee.

He spoke in his normal voice, but it felt like he was whispering in my ear. "Those Turks made swords so sharp they could slice in half a silk handkerchief thrown into the air."

I said, "Be careful."

"Why go to all that trouble for a sword?" Mother said. "Dead's dead, after all."

My father said, "You wouldn't understand," and winked at me, as if I did.

I singled my father out, she tried to make him blend in. We each thought our own method was best, and we never worked together. My mother's spell changed that. It allowed us to collaborate.

"Now he's switching off the office light," Mother went on, "thanking God no students followed him back there after class." She picked up her Oreo and considered it, as if it might tell her something.

I said, "He's going down the stairs." I saw him leaping gracefully, taking the stairs two at a time, like a dancing businessman in *Mary Poppins*.

Mother shook her head. "He closes his office door and locks it, because," she lowered her voice, "he hides his formula in there."

A sudden ratcheting snarl outside made us jump. A lawnmower had started up next door at the Loomises'. It was their grown son, Timothy, who still lived at home and couldn't keep a job. He had curly shoulder-length hair. From the back he looked like a beautiful girl, but from the front he looked like an old man in a wig.

"About time," Mother said, jerking her head in the direction of the Loomises' house. "I was ready to go over there with a sickle."

Timothy had recently tried to get me to go for a ride in his VW microbus with the peace sign on the door. "You won't believe my tape deck," he'd said. I'd been sitting up in my tree, my skinny legs dangling. "You're sexy," he said, staring at my flat chest. I knew he was lying, but I was flattered.

The light from the oak tree had slid across the kitchen floor and was lapping at my feet. "I need a new bathing suit," I told Mother.

"Not now," Mother said. "He's marching down the hall. He usually takes the stairs, for his heart, but now he decides on the elevator. Less chance he'll see Perkins or Hughes and have to exchange pleasantries."

"Smart move," I said, but I felt myself deflate. Getting him home was going to take a while.

"He pushes the elevator button. 'Ping,' the door opens. Behold!" Mother waved her soggy sandwich like a magic wand. "It's Bill Perkins!"

Bill Perkins was another professor in my father's department—my father's rival, and, in Mother's opinion, a blabber-mouth and a bore.

"Don't let Daddy get in."

"Ah, but he's already in, and the doors are closing. 'Hello, Allen,' says Perkins. 'Have I told you about my cruise?' 'Yesterday,' says your father, but Perkins goes through it all again. Your father watches the lights—3 . . . 2 . . . 1. The door opens, they get out, and Perkins is still yakking—yacht, French cuisine, sea turtles, blah, blah, blah."

I could no longer tell if Mother was merely reporting what she saw, or somehow causing it to happen. "Can't he get away?" I said.

"He steps squarely on Bill's toe. 'Oh, I'm sorry,' he says, and makes his escape."

"Perkins deserves it," I said, but I wasn't sure that he did. I'd never seen my father strike out at someone so directly, though I realized that the possibility had always been there, bubbling below the surface, and that on some level, I'd been aware of it. I watched his pant-cuffs, always a little too long, breaking on the tops of his shiny oxfords as he strode down the hall.

Mother went on, "Now he's pushing open that heavy door and stepping into the sunshine. He blinks like he hasn't seen daylight in forty years."

"He's off to the parking garage."

"The garage was full. He had to park on Summit. He's crossing Maple."

"He's walking fast." I saw his black briefcase, big as a suit-case, banging against his thigh.

Mother clapped her hands once, as if to remind me who was in charge of this vision. "He's walking slowly. Wonders if he forgot something, some article on that steel he wants to take on the trip." She took a sip of iced tea. "Okay, now he's walking faster. He thinks he left the article at home."

I scooted my chair back. "I'll see if it's in his study."

Mother grinned, amused that I was taking this so seri-ously. But I could tell that she also was taking it seriously. "Don't bother," she said. "That little article was misfiled acci-dentally on purpose. Eat your sandwich."

I did as she said, although I no longer had any appetite. The mayonnaise on my tongue made me uneasy.

"See what you made me do?" Mother said. This was one of my father's phrases and she glanced at me to see if I'd noticed. I curled up one corner of my mouth, and she continued. "You made me lose track of him. All right, I can see him now. He's already walked to the car. He's opening the car door, heaving his briefcase into the backseat. He climbs in. The car's broiling hot. He touches the dashboard. 'Ouch!' He touches the steer-ing wheel. 'Ouch!' He can't breathe, so he rolls down the win-dows."

"He's driving away."

"Not so fast. In through the window flies a sweat bee, one of those tiny little yellowjackets. It lands on the knuckle of his finger." She held up her pointer finger. "He doesn't notice.

He's thinking about the Damascus sword he cut up this morning and how he's going to duplicate what he found inside. Now he reaches down, sticks the key in the ignition, and zap! The bee stings him." She snickered, then covered her mouth as if she'd done something she needed to be excused for. She couldn't help herself. Pain spooked her, so she turned it into a joke.

The day before her magic spell, I'd stepped on a bumblebee. The stinger stuck in my bare foot, and I hopped three blocks home, howling, refusing to pick it out or even look at it. Mother followed as my father led me upstairs to their old oak bed. He pushed me down on my stomach and sat on my thighs, pinning me to the bed. I rolled and twisted, trying to kick my foot out of his reach. I was overreacting, but felt it was my duty to do so. He took off his glasses and handed them to my mother. I couldn't see his face, but I knew his cheeks were flushed, his lips tense, puckered. I kicked again, and he seized my foot and held it against his chest. "Hold still, you," he said, but he didn't mean it. He wanted the pleasure of subduing me, and being his daughter, I had to give it to him. My mother leaned over us, swinging my father's glasses by the stem, declaring she couldn't imagine what all the fuss was about.

Timothy Loomis's lawnmower roared closer as he took another turn outside the window. Mother folded her arms, genie-style, against her polka-dotted shirt. Her smooth face was forever untouched by fuss.

I rattled the ice in my glass. "It hurts, getting stung," I said.

"Just a pinch," Mother said. "He shakes his hand and says, 'What the hell?' But the bee's gone and he doesn't know what got him. He puts the car into gear and pulls out without looking."

I dug my fingernails into the plastic tablecloth. "He has a wreck!"

"The coast was clear. He does scrape the car parked in front of him, but that's not a wreck."

"Not a real wreck."

We settled back in our chairs. She'd set us up for nothing. A strange melancholy released us from her spell, and we both gazed out the window over the sink. The upper half of the window was full of stained-glass figures dangling from tiny suction cups—a hummingbird, a tulip, an old lady knitting in a rocker, a Cajun shack. Mother'd made them in a class she'd taken at the Y. When she hung them up, she'd said that she knew they were tacky, but she didn't have the heart to throw them away. My father never acknowledged them. I had always enjoyed their cheerful presence, but right then they appeared so optimistic I had to look away. The rest of our kitchen, with its butcher-block counters, Brookstone gadgets, and copper saucepans hanging in order of size from their hooks above the stove, seemed as calculated and insubstantial as a stage set. Mother and I were second-rate actresses, entertaining ourselves with a small drama until, with my father's arrival, the curtain rose and the main act began again.

I examined the grime underneath my fingernails, grime from the plastic tablecloth, grime that was always there no matter how hard I scrubbed the hideous red surface. I couldn't wait to get strange dirt on my hands, dirt from playing in the woods in Minnesota, dirt that would wash away when I dove, in a new Speedo suit, from the wooden dock into Eagle's Nest Lake. I couldn't wait to go canoeing with my cousins and sleep in a bunk bed on their screened-in porch. Mother and Aunt Minnie would spend their days playing double solitaire and drinking gimlets, and my father would have to spend his days fishing with Uncle Walter. The unfamiliar surroundings and activities and my cousins and aunt and uncle would be a layer of protection for me. I said, "Isn't it time he pulled into the driveway?"

Mother squinted up as though she could make out my father's image on the ceiling. "He's still on Summit. Now he makes a right on State."

In our white Oldsmobile with the maroon top, he whizzed

past the Big Cheese Drive-in. Mother said, "He's toodling down toward the levee, hoping there won't be a bunch of fools causing a traffic jam on the bridge."

"He's thinking that Timothy Loomis might burn our house down while we're gone," I said, pleased with the way his thought had popped into my mind.

"Is he?" Mother said, sitting up straight. "I do sense distress, but nothing so specific. More like his general pre-trip anxiety."

My father was a worrier. Before we left for our usual weekend at Brown County State Park, he would call everyone on the street—except the Loomises—to inform them of our departure and give them emergency phone numbers. He also checked the outlets and faucets. My job was to shut and lock all the windows, but I always left one in my bedroom open a crack, tempting something or someone, like Timothy Loomis, to sneak in and disrupt our lives. Meanwhile, Mother would sit in the passenger seat of the Oldsmobile, waiting for us and reading a copy of the tabloid she always treated herself to for car trips. While we traveled up Highway 41 she'd read the headlines aloud—"Egyptian Mummy Found with Live Cat" or "Ten-Year-Old Little Leaguer Gives Birth at Second Base," and then challenge my father and me to guess what the stories were really about. She never liked the macabre tales we came up with—she preferred the tabloid stories themselves. It tickled her that the details in them were so mundane—the cat's name was Maxine, the little leaguer lived in Monroe, Louisiana. Her habit of celebrating the folksy and tuning out the bizarre irritated me.

"Daddy hopes you'll forget your stupid newspaper this time," I said.

"Good guess," my mother said, raising one eyebrow. "But wrong. He's thinking about the angry letter he just got from the Smithsonian, telling him he's ruining valuable antique swords by cutting them up for research purposes."

I hadn't heard about this before. I wondered if my father had confided in her about it, or if she'd stumbled on the letter in his study. Either way, it was the sort of thing he wouldn't want me to know about. He was adamant about his privacy. I slumped down. "He won't do it anymore," I said.

Mother snorted. "Just because someone has pointed out the error of his ways?" *The error of one's ways* was another of my father's phrases. "He thinks he has a perfect right to cut up those swords. He bought them, after all."

"They'll take him to court," I said.

She pointed at my plate. "Want that cookie?"

"Don't touch it."

Mother watched me eat my Oreo, then she continued. "There he goes, zipping down State Street hill. He thinks he's going to make the light at the bottom, but it turns yellow just before he gets to the intersection. A coed on a scooter speeds around him."

"He slams on his brakes."

"He runs the red light, not about to let some little upstart get ahead of him. Hopes he won't get nailed." She drained her iced tea in one long gulp.

I'd never seen my father drive this way, but I had no trouble believing he would when we weren't with him. "Does he?" I said.

She set down the sweating glass. "Does he what?"

There was a grinding noise and then silence. Timothy Loomis had run over something with his lawnmower. His foot, I hoped. But no, in a few seconds he started the mower back up.

"Does he get nailed for running the light?" I nearly shouted.

"Not yet," she said. "He's heading toward the bridge, past that overpriced dime store, Sears and Roebuck."

"You like him to fix things," I reminded her, but without conviction.

On Saturdays, after we'd returned from Sears, my father spent the afternoon in his basement workshop refinishing furniture, framing a print, or rewiring an appliance, which he would later display in the kitchen for my praise and my mother's dismissive nod. Sometimes I sat on the stairs to observe him while he worked. He never spoke to me, but behaved as though he was aware of his audience. If he nicked himself with his glass-cutter or got a splinter in his thumb, he would let out a curse and hold his injured hand up to the bare lightbulb, so that I'd be sure to register the injury. He would turn his thumb slowly under the light, examining it, driving his point home. Finally, with a loud sigh, he'd start back to work. Why did he want my pity? Everything seemed to be calculated to an end that only he understood. I couldn't stand the sight of his pale neck, his slumped shoulders. I imagined him wreathed in smoke, ringed by beds of hot coals, his hands black with soot. Instead of fixing a toaster, he pounded a strip of glowing steel with his huge hammer.

"Uh-oh," Mother said. "The police. Coming up fast."

I pictured my father behind the wheel. I could see him clearly—his shiny white hair, his tortoiseshell glasses hooked behind his ears, the stubbly place on his jaw he always forgot to shave. "He pulls over," I said.

"Nope," Mother said. "He keeps driving toward the bridge. Playing the absentminded professor."

I saw him steering with one hand, humming and pretending to take in the scenery—the office buildings across the river, the church steeples in the distance. But I knew what he was thinking: "Let's see, where can I find a red-haired boy? Highland Elementary, of course. I'll stand behind a tree on the playground, and during recess I'll take note of the red-haired boys, and then after school I'll follow one. I'll offer him two dollars to pee in my glass jar."

I said, "The cop comes right up on his bumper." I could see the cop yanking my father out of his car, slapping handcuffs on him, shoving him into the back of the police car, my father protesting all the while.

"The cop swings around him," Mother said. "After some other poor sod. Maybe that girl on the motor scooter."

"He's off the hook," I said.

Mother eyed the clock. The big hand was at the base of the Matterhorn. One forty-seven. "Not entirely. I see trouble. There's young Mr. Hughes, hitchhiking on the bridge."

My father was of the old school—he called his students Mr. or Ms. in order to maintain the proper distance. But it didn't always work. Hughes, for instance, had been at Indiana State for years. He was my father's star graduate student and hung out constantly in my father's office. He showed up on our doorstep at odd hours, clutching another article about Damascus steel he'd just found, the article that was going to change everything.

"Does he give him a ride?" Daddy would feel obligated to.

"Your father," Mother said, "secretly hates Mr. Hughes. He wants to run him over. He wants to hear Hughes scream and see him fall backward over the railing, plunging to his death. No more dissertation committee meetings. No more conferences where Hughes does all the talking. But then, your father contemplates life in prison."

"He'd claim it was an accident."

"He decides not to kill Hughes. Not today. But he doesn't pick him up, either, even though Hughes sees him and frantically waves. Your father leans out the window and shakes his fist at Hughes." She grimaced and shook her fist.

I shrank back from her accurate imitation of my father's mean face.

She smiled, pleased with my reaction. "More tea? You can have half a glass."

"No." I resented the way she kept putting my father in situations from which she could rescue him.

Outside, the lawnmower sputtered to a stop. The silence

filled me with a dreadful excitement. I'd promised Timothy I'd go for a ride with him when we got back from our trip. He hadn't asked me not to tell anyone, but he knew I wouldn't.

In later years, I would picture myself, that dusty, wiry girl in the tree, her legs swinging, and I couldn't fathom why she would make such a promise, let alone act on it, when she cared nothing about riding in Timothy's microbus, when she found Timothy himself so frightening and repulsive. Now I think I know why, and it's simple really. She did it because Timothy wanted her to.

"When will Daddy the Great arrive?" I asked Mother.

"Soon, soon," Mother crossed her legs and swung her bare foot back and forth, and I had to move my chair to avoid contact with it. "Now he's zooming down Main, making all the lights," she said. "Wait, one got him. At Fifth and Main. He's idling there, beside the Downtowner. He smells food, which makes him hungry. That sexpot on the motor scooter comes up behind him and revs her engine. He switches on WRNA, hoping for Bartók, but it's pork bellies, which reminds him of the breakfast he had at the Downtowner this morning—sausage, eggs, and buttered grits. Thinks I don't know he eats his bran muffin at home and then hits the Downtowner for a second course."

"But what about his arteries?" I said.

"Exactly." Mother twisted around. The honeymoon clock read one-fifty, small hand on the goat's head, big hand in the mountain stream. "Just as his mouth starts to water, the sexpot taps her horn, politely, because the light's changed. He takes off, heading for the train tracks. So far, so good, but the warning lights start flashing. He accelerates. He knows we're waiting for him."

I saw the red and white gates descending. "We don't care that much if he's late," I said. "Do we?"

"Do we?" she repeated, insinuating that she knew me better than I knew myself.

"I don't." I kicked her swinging foot.

She paid no attention. "He's furious," she said. "Caught by a train. Today of all days. He doesn't even want to take this vacation with my stupid relatives and here he is racing around town risking life and limb. He pounds on the steering wheel."

I said, "Don't forget, your purple sweatshirt's in the dryer."

"He's going to try to beat the train. If he makes it, he'll feel like Superman. If he doesn't, then he'll show everyone. You, me, Perkins, Hughes, the Smithsonian, the sexpot. We'll all feel bad for how we've treated him." She looked at me, wanting me to stop her.

"Go on," I said.

"He guns it. He's racing down the street, imagining himself in the Indy 500. Sweat breaks out on his forehead. He stomps on the brakes at the crossing, making the tires squeal. He looks down the tracks, doesn't see the engine, holds his breath, and swings around the gate." She mimicked his neck craning, his hands twisting the steering wheel. "On the tracks he looks again." She turned her head and her eyes bugged out. "There's the engine. A monster with one headlight, bearing down on him. The engineer blows the horn." She made the sound of a horn, a terrible, blaring honk. "He doesn't have a second to waste, but he sits there thinking, 'I'm not ready to die! I'm so close to finding that formula. Perkins and Hughes will take over my work and get all the glory!' His heart is pounding. His foot fumbles for the accelerator . . ."

I stood up and screamed.

"It's okay," Mother said. "He makes it. Finish that cookie and let's clear the table."

"No, he doesn't," I said. "He doesn't make it." She'd brought us too far, or not far enough, and I wouldn't let her get away with it. I said, "His heart stops. He finally has a heart attack. He slumps over the steering wheel and the train tries to stop but it can't and it bashes into our car and Daddy's spattered into a million pieces." I sank down in my chair, put my arms on the table, and buried my head in them. "He's not coming home," I said. "He's never coming home." I felt a sickening, gleeful revenge.

Mother asked me, like a counselor, "Do you really wish your father was dead?"

"He is dead. We killed him."

"He's fine, silly. He'll be here any second." She squeezed my arm.

Mother and I had gone off, like I'd always feared we would, but it wasn't like skipping into a new groove on my fairy tales record. Instead we'd drifted slowly to this place, and although we'd never been here before, the island we found ourselves on wasn't strange or new. Mother had created it, yes, but she'd constructed it from existing materials, like our bones, intimately known, but hidden.

"There's the car now, see?" Mother said.

I kept my face buried and heard the tires of our Oldsmobile crunching to a stop on the gravel. "How did you know?" I asked her.

"I'm a witch." She giggled.

"You are not," I said, but I believed that she was. Years later, I wondered why my mother had never demonstrated her powers before that day, and why she never chose to use them again. And yet, I knew she didn't really have any supernatural powers, as she'd claimed, just insight and familiarity with her subject. But I do think some kind of magic happened. Mother started out by playing a game, but somehow, without intending to, she revealed a secret. Our desire to protect my father didn't spring from love, but from fear. We depended on him to keep everything in good running order, and we believed that because of him, we were a normal family. We went to church, we shopped at Sears, we took vacations.

"Just think," she said, her voice serene again. "Fir trees, cool mornings with mist on the lake, a fire in the fireplace."

"Loons," I said. My nose was smashed into the sour-smelling tablecloth. "Mosquitoes."

"Whiskey and lake water on the dock at sunset," Mother went on. "And a cherry Coke for you."

Had she really shifted back so quickly? I raised my head and saw that she hadn't. Her body was frozen in her chair, and her eyes kept blinking at nothing.

I said, "We almost didn't have a vacation."

Mother nodded.

Confusion squeezed tighter around us. We could have been any two people, stuck in an unfamiliar room, growing more and more uncomfortable.

The car door slammed.

Mother grasped what was required of her. She stood up and flung open the screen door. "Dearheart, you're home," she called, stepping out onto the porch. "What kept you?"

I heard Timothy and my father talking in the driveway, and then I heard my mother join in. The sound of their voices showed me the way back. I got up, cleared the table, and set our dishes in the sink. But instead of running out to greet my father as I usually did, I lingered there at the sink, my eyes drawn to the stained-glass figures in the windowpane. I leaned closer to the tulip, noticing beautiful bubbles in the purple glass. I reached up, unhooked the tulip from its suction cup, and slipped it into the pocket of my shorts. I wanted a memento of this occasion, because I knew Mother and I would never speak of it again.

Electric WiZard

T H R E E   W E E K S after Jason's death his father got hold of me on the phone. "Ms. Penrose? You were Jason's last teacher." It sounded like an accusation.

I wrapped the phone cord around my hand, wishing I'd let the answering machine pick up. "I'm so sorry," I said, hoping my apology would cover both Jason's death and my own lousy teaching. I stared down at the Turkish rug and for the first time I noticed little white nubs among the blue and green threads, as if it were aging as I watched.

"I'm calling to see if he might've said something," said Jason's father, whose name was Bishop. "Or done something. To indicate his state of mind." Bishop made a gulping sound—holding back a sob? Taking a slug of scotch? Jason was their only child. His death had been ruled a suicide.

I sank down onto the Turkish rug like a tent

collapsing. "He seemed fine to me," I said, which wasn't entirely true. Jason, a redheaded, rubbery-looking boy with knobby knees and black glasses, had been a student in my poetry writing class, part of a college camp for gifted kids. "I knew him for such a short time," I said, stretching out flat on my back. "I'm probably not the best person to ask."

"Did he write about anything, you know . . . ?"

I watched the blades of the ceiling fan go around and around and thought about the antique store in New Orleans where my ex-husband Grant and I bought the rug, a dim room full of low, ponderous ceiling fans and ornate mirrors. At that same shop Grant secretly bought a full-length mirror I'd been admiring and had it shipped home to Indiana to surprise me. Out of some stupid newlywed parsimoniousness I sent it back. "They all write about death," I said. "It's junior high." I cringed at the flipness of my words.

"The thing is," said Bishop. "He never showed us any of his poems. He must've thrown them all away." I heard the gulping sound again. It was like a chicken making a single cluck.

"I really can't remember what he wrote," I said, and then quickly added, "or the writing of any of my students. I've had so many." That wasn't true either. I remembered a poem written by a girl named Matisse about some passengers in a plane crash slowly drifting down toward the fields of southern Indiana. And Heather's poem about getting poison ivy. And my favorite, Watson's poem about God flunking his driver's test. But the unpleasant fact was that Jason hadn't written a single poem during the entire two weeks of my class. He'd played on the Internet during class writing time and I had let him do it, telling myself that the camp was voluntary, there were no grades, and I wasn't going to make both our lives miserable. Already I was spending six hours a day, glorious June days, shut up in a classroom with fifteen eighth-graders, something I did every summer to supplement my income from community college teaching. Usually the kids were eager and uninhibited and talented enough to make the whole thing worthwhile, but I'd had a few resisters over the years, and Jason was by far the most stubborn. Perhaps I sensed that his refusal to write was simply a strand in some larger tangle, and I certainly didn't want to start groping around, exposing things neither one of us was equipped to deal with. In any case, his failure to produce poems reflected badly on both of us, and I hoped no one else would find out.

Rain began to patter against the sliding glass door, and I turned my head from the fan to watch the rain. My girls were still at the swimming pool. "I've got two daughters," I said. "One's Jason's age. I worry about them all the time."

"Is anything coming back to you?" Bishop asked. "I need to know if he left any clues." According to a newspaper article, which quoted various friends and relatives, Jason had a fascination with death, with what a person would feel like right before he died. His parents had caught him playing at hanging himself before, the article said. But this time he'd electrocuted himself by dropping a blow-dryer into his bathtub. I thought, *playing* at hanging yourself? Why didn't his idiot parents commit him the first time? I wondered if maybe, since he was in the gifted and talented program at school, they thought he was just acting like a curious little genius.

I pictured Jason on the last night of camp, standing on one leg, storklike, in front of the auditorium full of eighth-graders, his intense voice, his poise, his lively pouf of red hair. "He read a poem at the Evening of Sharing and did a great job," I told his father. "It was our group poem, where each student wrote two lines and passed the work on to the next person. But I couldn't tell you which lines were his." I'd asked Jason to read the class poem because I felt guilty about our mutual failure, and his dramatic performance at the Evening of Sharing relieved some of my guilt. I began looking forward to teaching again the next summer, anticipating more success all around.

"What about his *own* poems?" Bishop said. "What were they about?"

It was raining harder, coming down sideways. The sheets I'd hung out on the deck railing to dry were getting drenched. "You're mental," Watson had told Jason once, in front of the entire class. Watson had twisted his flashy turquoise ring while leaning over Jason's desk. "He's just drawing pictures of the same little rat, over and over again." Jason had stared fiercely at his notebook, somebody in the back of the room had sniggered, and I'd gone on talking about line breaks.

"I think I remember one poem," I said. The lie was like one of my daughter's superballs careening through the house. I could only watch anxiously to see where the next bounce would take it.

"Yes?" said Bishop.

"It was about God flunking his driver's test."

"Could I see this poem?" Bishop said. "Could I get a copy of it?" I'd read in the paper that Bishop was a lawyer.

"I don't have it," I said. "I'm sorry."

"Maybe you can rewrite it."

"I don't think so," I said. "I really only remember the last two lines." Watson's poem was about an Italian man who was driving through the countryside and happened to see a chapel so beautiful it caused him to have a sudden religious conversion. Euphoric, he took his hands off the wheel and said, "God, will you drive?" and his car immediately crashed. "God flunked his driver's test." So the poem was about death after all—suicide, even—but since it was laughing at death, I hadn't noticed.

"Do the best you can," Bishop said. "We could come by tonight to pick it up."

"Not tonight," I said. If Jason's mother was as pushy as his father, I thought, no wonder the boy wanted out. And, of course, I hadn't been any comfort to him either. I chastised myself with a nasty little movie in my head—Jason, hanging back *again* after all the other students left class so he could walk out with me, refusing to talk to me or look at me directly, answering all my questions with a shrug. There I was, coaxing him along, trying to conceal my irritation, saying dumb, cheery things—"Maybe you'll be inspired tomorrow!" And there he was, frowning and finally turning away, scuffing off to the dorms alone. He electrocuted himself two weeks after camp ended.

"Tomorrow night then," Bishop said. "Around eight."

I felt cornered and wanted to strike. "Why do you think your son was so curious about death?"

"That reporter got it all wrong," Bishop said. "Jason wasn't fascinated with death. He was fascinated by magic. He was experimenting with electricity. He wanted to be a magician, like the Electric Wizard, Dr. Walford Bodie."

"Who?"

Bishop's voice changed to that of a carnival barker. "The Greatest Novelty Act on Earth! The British Edison!"

I didn't like the sound of this. "Never heard of him," I said.

"Dr. Bodie could pass six thousand volts through his body," Bishop said. "He could light up sixteen incandescent lamps, holding them all in his bare hands. The crowd loved him." Bishop laughed, but it sounded like a series of wild hiccups.

"I'll see you tomorrow night," I told Bishop.

At dinner, we hung our heads over pasta with Alfredo sauce. Olive, who had just turned twelve, kept tucking her hair behind her protuberant ears and sighing loudly between bites. When she was a baby I used to look at her ears and wonder if they'd ruin her life, but gradually I convinced myself that nothing would shake Olive's serene sense of self. No mere physical irregularity, anyway. She was tall and graceful and seemed to live in a higher, calmer sphere than the rest of us.

Maeve let a dribble of milk run down her chin and then

slurped it back up. She was eight. "Bernie Spaulding was talking about Jason at the pool today," she said. She had a round face and curly hair bleached by chlorine to the various colors of winter weeds. I was certain then that I knew the inner core of both of my children. Whenever I wanted to summon up the essence of Maeve, I thought about her on a sunny fall afternoon, a chill in the air. I saw her running through the front yard, kicking up leaves, wearing a red sweater. Olive watched her from upstairs, curled up in the window seat, *The Snow Goose* by Paul Gallico open in her lap. The essence of Olive.

Now Olive looked up from her plate, her face like a mask. "Bad things happen," she said in a flat voice. "Every minute of every day. Can we change the subject?" Jason's family lived in the town across the river from ours, so Olive and Jason had gone to different schools, but they'd met that spring at a science camp in northern Indiana. They spent a weekend together, collecting specimens of lake water and plants and examining them under high-powered microscopes, but Olive refused to tell us anything about him.

Maeve stirred her rigatoni vigorously. "Bernie said he was listening to the radio when he did it."

Outside, the rain was still coming down, splattering against the windows, but our painted furniture gave the room a gaudy glow. Five years earlier, after my divorce, I'd gone on a painting binge, transforming every surface available—furniture, lampshades, even the toaster—with bright colors, dots, dashes and squiggles and beads. Maeve liked the results, especially our dining table, which was Chinese red with a jagged Cree Indian design, but Olive was merely mystified. "How can you stand to make all those pointless dots?" she asked me. She had the same sort of reaction when I took up knitting and then fly tying. Her father, my ex-husband Grant, spent his days studying black bears in Minnesota, sneaking into their hibernation dens to change the batteries in their collars. He'd promised Olive she could go along with him this fall.

Grant would be baffled by the little dance that was now going on at our dinner table every night. Maeve and I compulsively discussed Jason's life and death—he'd built a treehouse with an elevator, he won the Soap Box Derby three years in a row, he'd put on swimming goggles before he got into the bathtub—and our conversations about him infuriated Olive. Her anger, as unexpected and irrational as our curiosity, only spurred us on. "What station do you suppose he listened to?" I asked Maeve.

"What difference does it make?" Olive said. "Morbid ghouls. Pass the salad."

I passed her the salad bowl, a cumbersome crystal thing we'd gotten as a wedding gift. I kept hoping it would break, but it never did.

"It was country western," Maeve said. "That's what Bernie said, anyway."

I said, "I can't picture Jason listening to Reba McEntire."

"Maybe he liked the newer country stars," Maeve said. "Like Travis Tritt."

"You don't know a thing about country music," Olive told Maeve. "Or anything about anything."

"Bernie also said he collected rubber knives." Maeve covered her mouth, and I wondered if she'd been making some of this up.

"You know," I said, giving Maeve a little wink. "I ran into the Grouts, Jason's neighbors, at the Food Co-op yesterday. I guess Jason's parents let his pigeons loose and they're taking over the neighborhood, pooping all over everything."

Olive glared at me. "Jason didn't have any pigeons."

Maeve looked up hopefully. "What'd he have?"

Thunder rattled the windows and the lights blinked off and then on again. Maeve and Olive froze, their forks in midair. The previous summer, lightning had struck our neighbor's tree and the current, snaking underground and invading our wires, blew our telephone right off the wall. I wanted to dive under the table, but I sat up straighter. "Did Jason have any pets?" I asked Olive, hoping to trick her with my matter-of-fact tone, but she just shook her head.

We all went back to our pasta, and I felt as if the three of us had always lived alone, eating our lonely dinners, the rain endlessly falling. Grant left us gradually, spending more and more time up north with his bears, until at last I realized that we were already separated. At this very moment a bear might be dragging Grant's lifeless body down the trail. How many weeks would pass before we found out?

Maeve tried again. "Bernie Spaulding said that Jason was naked, when he did it."

"He was taking a bath, stupid."

"Jason's parents are coming over tomorrow night," I told the girls, hearing the self-importance in my voice. "To talk about Jason. His father says he wanted to be a magician."

"Cool!" Maeve said.

Olive sighed and gazed at the ceiling.

"They want me to give them a poem of Jason's," I said. "And I don't have one."

"So?" Olive said.

Exactly, I thought, popping a caper into my mouth. I decided I wouldn't try to re-create the driver's test poem for Jason's parents. I still thought it was a brilliant poem, but to them it would seem silly and cynical, and besides, Jason hadn't written it. I would tell them the truth. Their son hadn't felt like writing, and I hadn't felt like making him write.

They rang the doorbell at ten past eight, introduced themselves as Willow and Bishop Bodman, and smiled briefly before letting their faces sag again. They looked vaguely familiar, the sort of people I often saw deliberating over peaches in the Food Co-op or hanging around the fringes of college functions and arts events.

One of them wore cologne that smelled like hot tea. Bishop was tall, well over six feet, with a scraggly red beard and wire-rimmed glasses. He wore baggy shorts, and sandals made of rubber and rope. Willow had a thin face and dark hair with an impertinent swatch of white near her temple. She wore a long rayon skirt with big red poppies on it, and I almost asked her where she got it. My own dress was black, because of the occasion.

I led them into the living room, where they sat gingerly on the edge of the sofa, as if they were in physical pain. It was getting dark outside, so I turned on a floor lamp, causing the colored beads I'd sewn onto the lampshade to rattle together. The Bodmans turned their faces toward me, irritated and expectant, expressions that reminded me of my girls when they were babies, waking too soon from a nap.

I settled down across from them in the room's most comfortable chair, feeling uncomfortable about taking it. "Let me say again how sorry I am," I said. "It's so awful."

They nodded as if I'd said something profound.

I forced myself to keep talking. "Jason was such a sweet kid. I feel lucky to have known him."

"Was he a good poet?" Willow said. Her large brown eyes blinked slowly. "I'm a teacher too," she added. "Fourth grade." She clasped her hands on her poppy skirt. "Do you think his work was publishable?"

"Well, sure," I said. "Eventually."

Bishop turned on his wife as if he couldn't help himself, as if he were a dog trained to attack. "What else can she say?" Then he glanced back at me. "Could I trouble you for something to drink? Maybe a glass of wine?"

Maeve, I knew, was lurking behind the kitchen door. "Honey, bring in three glasses of wine," I called.

Willow pushed her clasped hands between her knees. "I don't mean to put you on the spot," she said. "He wanted to be a poet, when he grew up. That's why I'm asking."

"Jason wanted to be a magician." Bishop's face flushed underneath the beard—the same way his son used to flush when I called on him in class.

In the kitchen, I could hear pans banging. I wondered what on earth was Maeve doing in there.

Willow fingered the beads on my lamp. "Very cree-a-tive," she said. "Jason painted coffee mugs in his spare time."

Just then Maeve entered the room, barefoot and dressed in a frilly pink party dress, one she never wore anymore because it was too tight. She was carrying an Egyptian-lacquered tray she'd dug out of some cabinet. The tray had a bottle of wine and three wine glasses on it. I hadn't meant for her to bring in the bottle—the wine was the cheapest grocery store kind.

"This is my daughter Maeve," I said.

Maeve nodded at our guests, set the tray down on the coffee table, and began to pour the first glass, hamming it up as if she were a waitress in some snooty restaurant. I wanted to yell at her, but I just watched, mesmerized. I'd never known her to behave in such a fashion.

"None for me," Willow said, suddenly sitting back on the couch.

"Then I won't have any either," Bishop said, and grimaced.

"Me either," I said, although I felt like guzzling the whole bottle. "Sorry, honey."

Maeve set the bottle down, picked up the full glass, and slid into the chair opposite mine, tugging the pink dress down over her thighs. She put her feet up on the coffee table and dipped her little finger into the glass.

"You can't drink wine," I said. "What's wrong with you?"

"I'm just holding the glass," she said, smiling like someone on a TV commercial.

"Here's the thing." Bishop fixed me with an intense look, so intense that I could feel myself shrinking back. "At the time of his death, Jason was researching Dr. Walford Bodie, the Electric Wizard. A great stage performer from the turn of the century. Dr. Bodie could run electricity through his body, thousands of volts, and not feel a thing, because he'd built up a tolerance."

Maeve was ogling Bishop, and I wanted to reach over and cover her ears.

"Dr. Bodie was against capital punishment," Bishop went on. "Really ahead of his time. He used an electric chair from Sing Sing in his act. He'd bring up a subject from the audience, hypnotize him, and then partially electrocute him right there so people could see the horror of it. He'd turn off the current just in time and slap the subject back to consciousness. It was very effective."

"Too bad you couldn't do that to Jason," said Maeve.

A terrible silence filled the room.

"Slap him back to consciousness, I mean."

Bishop filled one of the wine glasses on the coffee table, held it in front of him briefly, frowned, then set it back down again. His rubber sandal tapped frantically on the floor. The newspaper said he'd been the one who found his son in the tub.

Willow snatched up the wine glass as if she'd been waiting for him to put it down. "Jason had the soul of a poet," she told me, and took a sip. "Most poets are miserable, don't you think?" Her patch of white hair fell forward to conceal one eye.

"Oh, that's just a myth." I felt like she'd cornered me at a cocktail party I hadn't even wanted to come to.

"Aren't you a poet?"

Maeve watched us, entranced. She held her glass by the stem, and drops of wine spilled onto her dress.

"I used to write poetry," I said. "Back in graduate school. But then . . ." I waved my hand to indicate the house, my children. "I don't really miss it," I said. "You're supposed to miss it. But the desire to write poems just lifted from me, like a heavy cape."

"That's a poetic turn of phrase right there," Willow said. Her wine glass was empty.

Why had I used that pretentious simile? "I'm more of a dabbler now," I said.

"She ties flies," said Maeve. "She just made a really cool Bubble Pup."

"I do it for fun," I said, "and sometimes I use them in my teaching. One girl in Jason's class wrote a wonderful poem about a Red Quill. It was a very successful exercise."

"No it wasn't," Olive said. She was sitting on the stairs, and we all looked up. She peered down at us through the banister rails as if she were safe inside her castle, safe from our reprisal. "You told me that exercise flopped."

I grinned appeasingly, like a monkey. "That's my daughter Olive," I said.

Willow licked her lips. "Jason did free-writing in his journal every morning," she said.

Bishop snorted. "He never said anything important. He only wrote about food."

"Food's important," Willow said, but her voice lacked confidence.

Maeve offered her glass of wine to Willow. "A bear might eat my dad," she confided. "Maybe sixty pounds of him."

Willow accepted the glass with an awkward nod. "Sixty pounds of your dad is a lot." Then she turned back to me. "Is your husband a poet too?" She poured the wine down her throat.

"Ex," I said. "He's a wildlife biologist."

"Dr. Bodie wasn't just an entertainer," Bishop announced. "He used electricity to heal. He would connect himself to an electrical condenser and apply current to the patient with his bare hands."

"*Doctor* Bodie was a total fraud." Willow set down the second glass, now empty. "It was proven in a court of law," she said, her nostrils flaring. The white patch of hair made her look like a nervous piebald horse. Whoa, I thought.

"There were hundreds of witnesses," Bishop said, and made that awful gulping sound. "Sparks would fly, and a cripple would get up and walk again."

Willow shook her finger at Bishop. "You gave Jason that book because *you* wanted to be a magician. It was *your* book."

Bishop recoiled. Suicide or experiment, either way he could blame himself, but I didn't think she'd meant to blame him. She was just talking. "Jason had no more desire to be a magician than I do," she said.

"Do you?" Maeve said.

"Do I what?" Willow said.

"Want to be a magician?"

"It's just a figure of speech," I told Maeve, my stomach churning. Our conversation had come completely unmoored.

"Are you in third grade?" Willow asked Maeve, pouring herself another glass of wine.

"Why not drink straight out of the bottle?" Bishop muttered.

"She'll be in fourth," Olive said from her castle.

"What's seven dollars times eight dollars?" Willow said.

Maeve squirmed, blinking like she might burst into tears.

Willow faced her husband again. "If you'd wanted him to be a scientist, that would make sense. Or an inventor." She waved the glass of wine as if she were shooing a bug. "Hey! I've got a great idea for an invention. A toilet seat that comes down automatically after a man's used it! What do you think?"

Bishop covered his face with his hands.

I cleared my throat. "About Jason's poem," I said.

Jason's parents sagged back against the sofa, and their blind clawing at each other ceased. It's just the two of them now, I thought. They aren't parents anymore. A bubble of hysteria rose in my throat. What were they going to do? Nothing, apparently. They sat calmly, waiting to hear Jason's poem, and the weight of what had happened to them hung heavily in the room. I hoped they'd start fighting again. My resolution to be honest was seeping away.

"I could only recall the gist of that poem," I said, "so I didn't write it down. I would've been making some of it up."

"We don't mind," Willow said.

"Could you recite it right now?" Bishop said in what sounded like his courtroom voice.

"Maybe," I said. Why had I let these people into my house? I crossed and uncrossed my legs, trying to think of something to say about the Italian driver in Watson's poem—did he have a name? Why was he Italian? I couldn't form the first line in my brain.

Willow poured herself more wine. Bishop didn't seem to notice. He was staring at me.

I pointed at Willow's skirt. "I like your poppies," I said.

"She's thinking," Maeve announced, and scooped up an empty wine glass.

The silence in the room went on and on. Maeve began flicking the glass with her fingernail—tink tink tink. I told myself that I would be betraying Jason's spirit if I made up a poem on his behalf. But what about his desperate parents, who were right here in my living room? I closed my eyes and ordered myself to invent something meaningful and comforting and publishable, but I knew I didn't really need to. The Bodmans just wanted to hear a poem, any old poem, more than anything in the world, and I, who'd probably written a hundred poems, couldn't help them. I didn't trust my words not to reveal my own, and Jason's, inadequacies.

Bishop picked up the empty wine bottle by the neck, dangling it back and forth. "*Is* there a poem, or *isn't* there?" I could feel his anger billowing up again, this time surging toward me instead of his wife. In the lamplight his face faded in and out of focus, fuzzy and then too sharp. His glasses glinted in a scary manner. Was this anger the reason Jason couldn't write anything? I was having trouble breathing.

Finally Olive spoke. "Mother told it to me," she said. "I bet I can remember it."

We all turned toward Olive, who stood up on the stairs like she was preparing to deliver a speech. She wore one of her father's T-shirts, which hung past her knees, a T-shirt he'd gotten in the Mercy Hospital Road Race. RUN FOR FUN, it said.

"This poem is called 'Only Child.' " Olive took a deep breath. As far as I knew, Olive had never written, or even read, any poetry of her own free will. I wanted to rush up and silence her, but at the same time I couldn't wait to hear what she was going to say. "It's hard to be an only child," she began. "The laps I sit in disappear. Naked, I crawl forward, wondering why. Not caring if I live or die. Nobody knows me. They only know my name. And my test scores. Who's to blame?" She sat down abruptly, looking exhausted. "That's all," she said.

"There's a little more," said Maeve, rubbing her dry feet together. "Country music, rubber knives. The Electric Wizard's quite a guy."

"There was a line about God flunking his driver's test," I said. "Somewhere in there."

"Thank you," said Bishop, almost sheepishly.

"That bit about the laps disappearing," Willow said. "Breathtaking. Could you write the whole thing down?" she asked Olive.

"She doesn't need to." Bishop replaced the wine bottle in the exact center of the tray. "I have the information I need."

After Jason's parents left, the girls and I went outside and sat on the patio in our iron chairs. The lacy grillwork cut into my thighs. It was full dark—too cloudy to see the stars. There was a slight breeze blowing, teasing us with the faint smell of a neighbor's cookout, and fireflies were beginning to pulse all over the yard. It was too early in the year for cicadas, but I could feel their imminence, the sound that would signal the beginning of fall.

"Who is Dr. Bodie?" Maeve said. "How come I've never heard of him?"

"He's the Electric Wizard," said Olive. "Duh."

I slid down in my chair, hoping that Jason *had* been experimenting with electricity when he died. Had he been too caught up in his experiment to panic? It was the being shut out, the not knowing, that Maeve and I couldn't bear. Did Olive really not want to know? Maybe she was too afraid to even let herself wonder. I'd never had the courage to imagine what might lie beneath her reserve. Maybe I was as bad as Jason's parents, who'd seemed to think that his suicidal behavior arose from sheer genius.

"Why couldn't I drink the wine?" Maeve asked me. She looked like a small pink ghost in the big chair. "Why couldn't I even taste it?" she said. "Are you afraid I'll turn into an alcoholic? If I did I'd join AA."

She was fluid, assured—a bit of a ham. She might become an actress, I thought, and the thought disturbed me, mostly because it was something I'd never even considered.

"Being an alcoholic is no joke," Olive said, drawing her knees up underneath her T-shirt. "It's not something to laugh about. I think Jason's mother is one. She drank the whole bottle of wine."

I was probably dutybound, as a mother, to deliver a lecture on either drinking or lying, but at the moment neither one seemed important. Something between us had cracked open, and I wasn't ready for it to close. "That was really amazing, what you did in there," I told Olive. "Where'd that poem come from? It *was* breathtaking."

"It was really about me."

Maeve slapped a mosquito on her calf. "You're not an only child, honey-pot," she said.

But she is a child, I thought. The same age as Jason. She's the one who would know, if any of us could, the worries and fears he might've had. I asked her, pleaded with her, "Don't you care whether you live or die?"

She hugged her legs tighter, her pointed chin resting on her knee. "If something happens to Daddy, I might not care. Or to you."

Her words hit me like a jolt, and I ached to reassure her, to cover up, to make light, but for the moment I resisted. I remembered the Italian man, lifting his hands from the wheel. God, can you drive? I was already bracing myself, bracing for the crash. But I also knew that most changes don't begin with a crash. They start in quiet places like that strange New Orleans shop filled with fans and mirrors, and they continue gradually, for years, and we don't even notice. I glanced at the glowing hands of my watch.

"Jason showed me a magic trick," I said. "Did I tell you?"

"No," they both said, but in completely different ways.

"Hold my hands," I said.

We sat there for a few seconds and then, at exactly 9:35 P.M., our neighbors' security lamp came on. "See, it worked," I said.

"Wow!" Maeve said.

"Could just be a coincidence," Olive said.

Our yard pulsed with an eerie greenish light, illuminating our tomato plants, our cracked marble birdbath, our joined hands, a spectacle that might have inspired the Electric Wizard himself. I wanted to gather it all in, to capture and hold it somehow, and keep us for a while just as we were, before we became whatever it was we were going to be.

The Visible Man

BY THE time Rona Arbuckle arrived to pick
Althea Fish up for lunch, Althea had almost given
up. She was sitting in the lobby of the Sycamore
Retirement Villas, and had just decided to walk back
to her room and go back to bed when she spotted
Rona's Saab idling in front of the building. In the
pale spring light the red car looked like a glaring
mistake. Althea closed her eyes. She didn't want to
see Rona, but she hadn't had the energy to call and
decline her invitation, delivered yesterday by mail, a
silly little YOU ARE INVITED card. Earlier that morning it had taken all of Althea's willpower to lift the
spoon and eat her Bran Buds, peel off her flaccid
nightgown, and rake a comb through her hair, which
used to be silvery blond but was now the color of a
used cigarette filter.

"Hey there!" She felt talons gripping her shoulder. "Thea. You asleep?" Rona was sixty years old but still had the look and demeanor of a cheerleader, one who'd seen too much overtime but felt obligated to keep on cheering. On weekdays she wore business suits, but today she wore what she called "play clothes"—white shorts, a navy cotton sweater with a white sailboat on it, white socks, and navy tennis shoes. Althea had never realized till this moment how much she disliked nauticalia—was there such a word?

Rona sat down in a turquoise chair that matched Althea's. Sycamore Villas had recently been redone in Southwestern style, even though this was Indiana. They'd painted everything peach and turquoise, hung paintings of cliff-dwelling Indians on the walls, and propped a withered cactus up in the corner of the lobby. "You didn't tell me you'd be waiting down here," said Rona. "Are you hiding something in your room? Like a dead body?" This was Rona's idea of a joke. Althea had endured jokes like this for the fifteen years she'd cleaned Rona's house. Every Friday, over lunch, she'd listened politely to stories about severed heads and ghosts and killer bees.

"I'm not hiding anything," Althea told Rona, but in a way, she was. Her room was as institutional and barren-looking as this waiting room, and she was ashamed of it. Most of the things she'd kept when she moved to Sycamore Villas nearly a year ago were still in boxes underneath her bed. Rona would insist on helping her unpack everything. For some reason, Rona wouldn't leave Althea alone. She'd visited her in the hospital and took her out to Wendy's on her seventieth birthday. She called every week to ask how Althea was feeling. How would anyone feel? Max was dead and she was living in a state nursing home.

"I talked to your psychiatrist yesterday. Dr. Wong?" Rona patted her knee. "I told him that if your new medication doesn't work, he should try shock treatment. But *don't* worry about it. Shock treatment's a lot less brutal than it used to be. Plus, it works!"

Rona would never understand that things like medication,

shock treatment, and foreign doctors went right through Althea without causing a ripple. What worried her were the small things, like the red thread now dangling from her skirt. "Do you have scissors?" she asked Rona.

Rona gave her a sideways, calculating look. "You mean on me?"

Althea lifted the string to show her why she needed them.

"Sharp objects are probably not a good idea," Rona said. "When you're feeling so bad." She stood up, grabbed Althea's hand, and jerked her to her feet as if she wanted to surprise her into action. "My chariot awaits," she said, and began pulling Althea toward the door. "Oh my God, you forgot your shoes!"

Althea wore an old pair of Max's argyle socks. She hadn't forgotten shoes—they were just too much trouble to put on. And why bother, when she was just going from the lobby to Rona's car, into her house for an hour, and then back here again?

She could almost hear Rona's mind working. *It might take a good thirty minutes to get a pair of shoes and convince Althea to put them on.* Rona bent over and untied her own tennis shoes, pulled them off and then her socks. Her feet looked dingy after the sparkling white socks. "I'll keep you company," said Rona. "If they arrest one for indecent exposure, they'll have to arrest both of us."

Soon they were zipping down the bypass in Rona's car. It was a sunny, peppy day, the trees sporting brand-new leaves. Rona looked like a child behind the wheel, and her bare feet only magnified this illusion. She'd always given Althea a ride home on Fridays, and she always drove too fast and hit the brakes too hard, which made Althea queasy, but it was better than taking the bus. Now Rona was talking about what she'd be serving for lunch—chicken salad and brownies with vanilla icing. And coffee. She said she knew how much Althea liked coffee, when actually, Althea only drank it to distract herself from Rona's incessant chatter. Rona always served it with horrible-tasting evaporated milk. "I'm evaporating," Althea said.

"What?" Rona stepped on the brakes and then on the gas. "Of course you're not!" she said. "That's just your depression talking." Rona gave Althea's arm a squeeze. "We're going to have a nice lunch, like in the old days, just the two of us. There's something I want to talk to you about, because *you* never tell me to stop imagining things."

Uh-oh. This wasn't good. Althea felt down around her knee for the thread, wrapping it around her finger. The car swung right onto Park Street, a narrow street lined with bungalows and picket fences, the street Althea and Max had once lived on.

"Want to see your old house?" Rona asked.

That would mean making a U-turn, which Rona would do in a gleeful, reckless manner, so Althea said no, even though she desperately missed her former home, a craftsman-style house she'd been forced to sell before she went into Sycamore Villas. By the time Max died of brain cancer, all their savings were gone, even though they'd had insurance through the university, where Max had worked for thirty years on the buildings and grounds crew.

"Take me to the cemetery," Althea said.

"Now now," said Rona. "You're not dead yet."

"I have to get out of that place," Althea said.

"I know you. You'll grow to love it there!" said Rona. "And you've got that nice blind friend."

Althea didn't have a blind friend, but she didn't bother to correct Rona, who would only insist that she did. Dr. Wong was no help either. Yesterday, when she'd said the same thing to him, "Get me out of that place," he'd just laughed like she was telling a joke, scribbled out her new prescription, and ushered her to the door.

Rona was still talking. "I knew women who had shock treatment just for fun. Back in my hometown." Rona was from Alabama somewhere, and Althea wasn't surprised to hear about anything people did down there. "You know, Seth has been seeing Dr. Wong too," said Rona, as if this would be a comfort to Althea. "He's on antidepressants now."

Last Althea remembered, Rona's son Seth still lived in town and did some sort of clerical work at the hospital. Rona'd been divorced since Seth was little, and often complained about it—"We single moms have a tough time"—putting herself in the same category as the welfare moms down on Fourth Street, even though she was a dean at the university. Max and Althea had never been able to have children, which sometimes felt to Althea like a terrible loss and sometimes like a ghastly fate barely avoided.

Rona made a left turn in front of an oncoming pickup truck, which blared its horn in protest. "Seth just moved out, into his own apartment," said Rona. "I've given up on him going to medical school. But he's got a new girlfriend, an anesthesiologist. Can you beat that?"

"No," said Althea. She'd suspected for years that Seth was a homosexual. Even in high school, he never seemed to have any interest in impressing girls. Rona was always talking about some girl or other who was *after* Seth, so Althea sensed that Rona knew too, but would never admit it.

Rona said, "Seth brought his new gal by the house last week. Her name's Serenity. Isn't that a hoot? Seth and Serenity. She's got a big mouth. I don't mean she talks a lot, I mean her mouth's big." Rona took her hands off the wheel and stretched her lips wide. The car drifted toward a telephone pole till Rona finally caught it. "I'm already planning their wedding!" Rona said. "I can't say that to anybody but you. Isn't it funny how I can talk to my *cleaning* lady better than my friends?"

Who was she kidding? Althea thought. Rona didn't have friends. She and Althea certainly weren't friends, but what were they? There wasn't a word for it. Althea had become one of Rona's projects, like curbside recycling or Mothers Without Partners. And Rona was Althea's ticket out of Sycamore Villas, if only for a few hours.

The car was now winding down Highland Avenue, a wide brick street of mostly Victorians. As the familiar houses slid past, Althea greeted them one by one.

"There's something that bothers me about Seth's wedding," Rona said. "I'll have to dance at the reception. I'm a terrible dancer. I'll look like a fool! The thought of it makes my skin crawl." Rona wheeled into her driveway and slammed on the brakes. "Here we are," she said.

Althea looked around. She hadn't seen Rona's house for two years, and she realized she'd never said a proper good-bye to it. The place looked peaceful as always, a two-story Colonial made of white limestone bricks, surrounded by tall maple and oak trees. The same green haze of mold lined the house. The little pond was still there in the front yard, but now it was empty. Seth used to fill it full of various creatures—mostly tropical fish that died or frogs that hopped away. But the grass was newly mowed, and the pink peony bushes were in full sugary bloom. "I'm just going to sit here," Althea said.

Rona sighed, her irritation finally showing. "You walked out to the car just fine. Do you want me to take you back?"

Althea thought about this. She didn't want to walk inside, but she also wasn't quite ready for another car ride with Rona. Strangely enough, she felt as if she and Rona had just arrived home after a long journey together. Before she knew it, she'd opened up the car door and was standing in the driveway. Her finger ached, and she lifted her hand and noticed the red string wrapped tightly around it. She hadn't needed scissors after all.

"Your medication must be working," said Rona. "What are you taking now?"

"Can't remember," said Althea. But she did feel sprightly, walking toward the door. How many times had she walked to this door from the bus stop, slipping on ice, sweating in the humidity? She'd always told herself she merely tolerated the job and found Rona profoundly irritating, so why was she now feeling a tickle of anticipation? Maybe it was just the medication.

Inside, the house smelled and looked the same. If Althea was placed blindfolded in the living room of this house—unlikely, but you never know—she'd recognize her surroundings by the smell: a closed-up, sweetish, antiseptic kind of smell. The furniture was still the same, the impractical white couch and citrus-colored silk chairs. Everything looked clean, even the pale green carpet had no footprints in it. Just looking at the carpet made Althea want to lie down. It was a leftover feeling from her cleaning days, when she spent much of her time alone, fighting to keep from sinking down onto beds and couches and nice soft carpets. Now she unwound the thread from her finger and dropped it. Who was vacuuming now? Was there a new Althea? She thought about asking, but Rona had her by the shoulders.

"Let's go right on in and I'll serve you up some lunch," Rona said. They crossed the foyer and stumbled into a mound of laundry on the floor. "Seth," said Rona, kicking the clothes down the stairs. "I guess Serenity's too busy knocking people out to do his laundry. Did I tell you she's an anesthesiologist?" Rona steered Althea up to the kitchen table and into a chair. "We're in for a treat," she said. "Any excuse for chocolate. You know me."

The kitchen floor looked dull—wax buildup—but there was a new tablecloth on the table, a festive print of Parisian street scenes. Somebody else must've picked it out, Althea decided. She was pleased to see that the sink was full of dirty dishes. Rona's rebellion.

Rona opened the refrigerator door and began rummaging around. "I've lost touch with the contents of my refrigerator," she muttered.

On the tablecloth, Althea noticed, it was the same little street scene repeated over and over again. The same little Eiffel Tower, over and over. She stood up, feeling woozy. "I'm going to the bathroom," she announced, and started out of the room, pleased with the way her sock feet took her smoothly along, out of the kitchen, moving under their own power. In the foyer, she paused. The bathroom she'd be expected to use, the guest bathroom, was downstairs, but she decided to go upstairs instead. Upstairs, she stood for a minute in the bathroom, flushed the toilet, then peeked into Seth's room.

Everything was just as she remembered it. Seth's posters of constellations and fossils still hung on the walls, his encyclopedias still lined the bookshelf, his scientific toys were still stacked on the desk. When Seth was a kid he'd pestered Althea while she was working, following her from room to room asking her idiotic questions—Would she care for a *delicious bar of Ex-Lax?* Would she like to play *52 Pickup?* But as he grew older he became silent and almost wary, lying on his bed pretending to read *Scientific American* while Althea cleaned his room. Every week she enjoyed dusting his microscope, his junior chemistry set, and the glass cover of his insect collection, which had earned an A-plus in ninth grade. He also had an anatomy kit called the Visible Man, a model of a human figure with clear plastic skin so you could view his skeleton and color-coded organs. She could still see Seth bent over his desk, diligently assembling the Visible Man, painting the veins blue, the rectum green, the liver red, the brain white, then hooking the bones together, slipping the organs into their correct cavities, snapping the breastplate on. When he finished, he stuck the man back in his box—even though there was a display stand included—which struck Althea as disrespectful. Sometimes, when Seth wasn't around, Althea would open the box, detach and examine the organs, and then try to replace them without consulting the instruction manual, feeling a strange thrill when she could. She loved the scientific names, the thin rivers of blood, the clarity.

Now Althea tiptoed over to the desk and began pawing through the toys, looking for the Visible Man. There was his cardboard coffin, on the bottom of the stack. Hands shaking, she pulled out the box and peeked inside. Underneath his sheer skin, his organs were all in their proper places. Liver, colon, testes. His penis was just part of the clear outer shell, which Althea felt was cheating. She gave his penis a little squeeze, but it didn't seem to bother him. His skeleton face grinned away at nothing; his red eyeballs stared. She'd remembered him as a proud and splendid creature—a Wall Street tycoon—but today he looked more like the victim of a plague. A jaunty victim. Typhoid Larry. All he needed was a bandanna and a jug of rum.

"Thea! What on God's earth?"

Althea closed the box and turned around. Rona stood in the doorway. "Are you all right? Did you forget what you're doing?"

"I came in here to clean," said Althea, shaking her head as if it were fuzzy. "But I forgot my dust rag." She set the box back on the desk.

"Honey, you don't work here anymore," said Rona, marching over to escort her back downstairs. "You are here as my guest."

Althea stole a look back at the box and wished she'd thought to bring her purse up here with her, her purse which was really a big string shopping bag. Rona'd never miss him, she decided. And he'd be much happier with her.

Down in the kitchen, Rona had laid out chicken salad on beds of lettuce and served it on glass plates with the outlines of grape leaves on them. The veins of the leaves reminded Althea of the veins in the Visible Man.

Rona speared a hunk of chicken salad. She frowned and spoke slowly. "Are you having trouble with your memory?"

"What memory?"

Rona barked with laughter. "Have you told your Dr. Wong about it? He might have to adjust those meds."

Althea took a nibble of the salad. "Too much mayo," she said, without realizing she was speaking aloud.

"Oh well," said Rona, her feelings clearly hurt. "It came

from Marsh deli." She lowered her head and began to shovel it in. After a moment she bobbed back up. "Met another PH last Saturday at the car wash," she said. "False teeth, but he drives a Jeep." PH meant Potential Honey, an expression she'd picked up on campus.

Althea wished she didn't know Rona's vulnerabilities so well. Even though Rona had a Ph.D. and an important job, her life was barely in control. She was always trying to diet. She couldn't cook or clean, and she was always flailing out against loneliness. "I asked him to teach me how to dance," Rona went on. "He said 'no can do.' Don't you just *hate* that expression? 'No can do.' What a fuddy-duddy." She sighed melodramatically, gazing heavenward. "I'll never learn to dance," she said.

"Take a dance class," said Althea, knowing Rona never would.

"Good idea!" said Rona. "Althea, you're a genius." She nibbled on some lettuce. "Where would I do that?"

"How about Arthur Murray's?" said Althea. When they were first married, she and Max had lived in a tiny apartment above the Arthur Murray Dance Studio. On weeknights Althea would come home from her job at Loeb's Department Store, kick off her pumps, toss her red wool coat on the bed, and she and Max, who was usually still in his sweaty work clothes, would dance along with the big band music coming up through their floorboards, Count Basie or Duke Ellington, following the dance instructor's directions as best they could, often falling into a laughing heap on the floor. "Look at me!" the dance instructor would shout at his students. "Look at me!" Little Brown Jug. Chattanooga Choo-Choo.

"Is Arthur Murray's still in business?" Rona said. She wiped her lips and folded her napkin. "Arthur Murray. Now there was a homely man. People on TV were uglier back then, don't you think? Not just him and his wife. Red Skelton, Milton Berle, Sid Caesar. All hideous."

Rona went on talking, and Althea found herself thinking about the Visible Man, imprisoned in his dusty box, and how she was going to manage to get back upstairs, with her purse, and slip him inside. In all her years of cleaning houses, she'd never had the desire to take anything before now, in part because she'd always thought of the houses she cleaned, and their contents, as belonging, in a way, to her. She was like the poor sister who popped in and out of her stepsisters' lives and carried the details back to Max. He loved hearing about the cat couple, who scolded her if she turned on the vacuum cleaner without first calling out, "Kitties! Althea's gonna make a vroom-vroom!" And the family of tall, handsome tennis players who held belching contests and had dock spiders in their basement. Without Max at home to help her put Rona in perspective she felt vulnerable, endangered. The Visible Man seemed like something to cling to, a familiar plank to keep her afloat.

"I hope Serenity wants to have children," Rona was saying, "but I hope they look like Seth. Do you think it would be premature for me to buy a crib? Not to give them. I'd put it in Seth's room. For when they visit. Who could take offense at that?"

"Seth could."

Rona blinked, startled, and went back to her salad. Althea wondered why she rarely told Rona what she really thought. For some reason, she felt more like being honest since she'd decided to steal something. She said, "I *like* it when people say 'no can do.' "

"Huh?"

"No can do. One of my favorite expressions."

"Okay. Sure. Well. Anyway." Rona pushed her plate impatiently aside, as though it were imposing on her. "I've got something to tell you," she said, glancing quickly around the room. "*My house is haunted.*"

Althea said nothing, so Rona continued. "I don't even believe in ghosts, but I've got one. A mean one. When it's quiet I can hear him breathing. Last week I found all my black socks wadded into one big ball. Isn't that creepy? Sometimes I can smell waffles, and I haven't fixed waffles in years. I *despise* waffles. And this morning I almost slipped in a puddle of water in the hallway. At least I think it was water. *And I don't know how it got there.*" Rona gazed at Althea intently. "But here's the worse thing. Know how you feel pressure when someone sits down on your bed? Sometimes I feel his hand on my knee. Not a friendly feeling. It's like he's planning to attack me." She pursed her lips. "*Rape* me."

Althea forced herself to keep chewing the tasteless chicken. She did a quick mental inventory of Rona's obsessions over the years—was this one the most absurd ever? Yup. She pulled her purse up into her lap. "How could a ghost rape?" she asked Rona.

"Good question," Rona said. "But I feel like this one could manage it." She popped out of her chair and opened up a cardboard carton on the counter. "I'm going to start on dessert!" She cut herself a large slab of brownie, poured herself a cup of coffee, and sat back down. "I'm too scared to sleep at night," she said. She tried to smile as she chewed. "I finally got your Wong to prescribe me some knockout pills."

"He's not *my* Wong," Althea said. "And he's a scumbucket."

"Well," said Rona. "I don't know about that." She took a dainty, professional-woman sip of coffee.

Underneath the table, Althea began fumbling around in her purse, wondering if the Visible Man would fit inside. She could dump the contents of her purse into the wastebasket if she needed to. It would be worth it. "I think I'll go right to dessert too," she said.

"Oh. Sure." Rona hopped up to cut Althea some brownie.

"Could I have some of that delicious evaporated milk with my coffee?"

"Why certainly!" Rona disappeared into the pantry.

Althea leaned over the huge Rubbermaid wastebasket, opened her purse, emptied it, and sat back down before Rona returned, triumphantly bearing a can of milk.

Rona served Althea coffee with yellow milk curdling in the center, and a hunk of brownie, and Althea said, "Thanks so much." She had no idea what she'd just thrown away. The only thing she might miss was her Social Security card. But how was she going to get back upstairs and rescue the Visible Man?

Rona dropped heavily into her chair. "I keep on thinking," she said, "of this religious pamphlet I once got handed on campus, asking 'Are you bugged with fear?' " She swung her arms out, knocking over her coffee cup, spilling coffee all over the table. "Phooey," she said, and jumped up, fumbling at the roll of paper towels. "I'm hoping you can help me."

"Me?" said Althea, squeezing her empty purse. "I'm a certified basket case."

Rona laughed gaily, blotted coffee into a Parisian street scene, and tossed the wad of paper towels onto the counter. "I've got to get rid of this ghost." She gazed beseechingly at Althea. "I thought we could have a little séance thing."

"A séance thing?"

"Just a quickie," Rona said. "Ask him to tell us what he wants."

Althea had never been in a séance before, only seen them on TV. She had no idea how to conduct a séance. "How about in Seth's room?" she said.

"Seth's room?"

"I think the conditions are good in there."

Rona clapped her hands. "I knew I was asking the right person. Finish your brownie and let's go."

Upstairs, Rona lit two candles and placed them on Seth's bedside table—white candles in brass candleholders. Vanilla-scented. They sat down across from each other on Seth's twin beds, which were neatly made with red corduroy spreads. His Boy Scout sash, thick with badges, was slung over one bedpost.

"Wouldn't it be better in my room?" said Rona.

"No," said Althea, looking over at the Visible Man. "You'd better pull the blinds." The box was far too big for her purse, she realized. What had she been thinking? Her purse lay on her lap, empty but useless.

When the room was dimmer they sat there foolishly, waiting for something to begin.

"Hear him breathing?" whispered Rona.

"I think that's the central air."

"No it's not," Rona snapped, and then, more plaintively, "Listen. It's deep, like a growl."

Althea did hear something now, something like breathing, soft and steady. She pictured the Visible Man's lungs rising and deflating.

Rona whispered, "What next?"

"We close our eyes," said Althea, who opened hers to make sure Rona had obeyed. She had.

"Yes?" said Rona, as if she were in a trance.

Althea glanced at the Visible Man. Then she sat up as straight as she could. "I'm getting a message," she said.

Rona wrinkled her nose. "What's it want?"

"No talking," said Althea. "It's not an it. It's a person. A man."

"A young man?" said Rona.

"No," Althea said sternly. "An old man. Very old."

"Can I say something?"

"Make it quick."

Rona's eyes popped open. She was sweating, wisps of blond hair curling up around her face. "Why's he so angry at me?"

"Silence," said Althea. "Close your eyes."

Rona did as she was told, and Althea suddenly knew two things—first, she'd only been invited to lunch today because of the ghost, only because Rona wouldn't parade her neuroses in front of anyone else; and second, she would not be invited back again.

"I can see the ghost now," said Althea. "He's sitting there beside you, on the bed."

"Where?" Rona stiffened up like a charmed cobra. "What's he doing?"

"Drinking rum, from a jug. He has the other hand on your knee."

"Make him stop," said Rona. She let out a little whimper.

"Okay, he stopped," said Althea. "Now he's wiping his eyes with his handkerchief. He's sad because he misses Seth. He only came here because he was attracted to Seth. Being a homosexual himself. He'd never rape you."

Rona sighed. "That's a relief," she said.

Althea felt a stirring in her chest like a swarm of bees. Something was happening. When she spoke again, her voice sounded deeper and louder, like Typhoid Larry's voice would sound, if he had one. "There is something you should know."

"What's that?"

"Your son is a homosexual."

Rona hunched her shoulders and screwed up her face as if it had started raining, hard, right into her eyes. Acid rain. "But he's going to get married," she said. "In the arboretum."

The buzzing in Althea's chest stopped abruptly and she felt her body sag. It's no use, she thought. Then she heard footsteps coming down the hall. There *was* a ghost!

The door swung open and Seth stuck his head inside. He needed a haircut. "What are you doing in here?"

"Want some lunch?" said Rona.

Seth stepped into the room. He looked as handsome as ever, with his dark eyes and square chin, but over his T-shirt he wore a pale blue down vest. Althea had always wondered who would wear such a useless and ugly piece of clothing. "Hello, Seth," she said.

"You remember Mrs. Fish?"

"Of course. Hello." He didn't smile. "Why are you in my room?"

"We just now came in," said Rona, clasping her hands together as if she were going to pray.

Seth flipped on the light and glanced at the candles. "You were having a séance. You were trying to contact that damn ghost. Don't deny it." He folded his arms on his chest.

Rona smiled her cheerleader smile but said nothing.

Althea said, "We did contact the ghost." She blew out the vanilla candles with great gusto.

"Honey, the ghost is a *pirate*," said Rona.

"His name's Typhoid Larry." Althea tried to speak casually, like she was introducing the mailman. "He's gone now. He had things to do—murders, plundering."

Seth frowned at Althea, looking her up and down, his eyes finally resting on her argyle socks.

"Seth," said Althea. "I hear we have the same doctor now. Good old Dr. Wong. Isn't he a card?"

Seth turned back to his mother. "Do you tell *everyone*?"

"Only her. Swear on a Bible."

"I practically forced it out of her," Althea said.

Seth waved his hand. "Listen. I just came by to give you some news. I'm going to take a job in Brisbane, at the Royal Victoria Hospital. That's in Australia." He nodded as if confirming his good sense of geography. "It starts in two months."

Rona said, "I can't believe it."

"Well, you better believe it," said Seth, with the bluster, Althea thought, of someone who doesn't know what the hell he's doing.

Rona seemed to have shrunk into a smaller version of herself. "What about Serenity?" she said in her new small voice.

"What about her?"

"You'll break her heart."

"How many times do I have to tell you? We are *just friends*."

"Good friends?"

Seth shook his head and his neck turned red.

"Listen," said Althea. "Isn't it too warm out for the vest? It's such a warm day."

Seth looked down and plucked at his vest as if he were surprised to see it. "It's not that warm," he said.

Rona took a deep breath, inflating herself back up to normal size. "Honey. That ghost said you were a homosexual!"

Seth opened his mouth, made a sound like a horse snorting, turned, and left the room, stomping off down the hallway. "*I am not!*" he yelled, thumping down the stairs.

"Don't forget your laundry!" Rona called, but the back door slammed shut.

Rona and Althea smiled wanly at each other.

"I already bought a dress for their wedding," said Rona. "Lavender with yellow blossoms." Her expression was one Althea'd never seen on her face before—empty, as if she'd gone and checked into a new hotel, into a room where no one could reach her.

Come back here, Althea wanted to say.

Rona sank back on the bed and lay stiff and unmoving, gazing at the ceiling.

After a while Althea said, "Can I get you something? Coffee? Another brownie?"

Rona curled up her toes. "No. Thank you."

It wasn't just that Seth was moving halfway around the world, Althea realized. Rona saw Serenity as her last chance. Her only chance.

"I'm sure Seth will meet another girl," said Althea. "A nice Australian girl."

Rona sniffled and covered her face with her hands.

"He'll find one prettier than Serenity," Althea went on, feeling like a fool but quickly warming to the feeling. "A girl with a small mouth. Who loves to do laundry." And so he might, Althea thought. So what if he is a homosexual? What did it matter? A lot of those marriages seemed to work out anyway.

Rona wouldn't say anything. The sailboat on her chest rose and fell too quickly.

"They'll get married in the arboretum," Althea said, "and it will be a sunny day, like today, and you'll be standing under the gazebo in your lavender dress, sipping champagne with your new PH. One who has a Jeep *and* teeth. You'll be watching Seth dance with his beautiful Australian bride. His already pregnant Australian bride."

Rona still didn't respond, and Althea feared she'd gone too far. Then Rona uncovered her face and wiped tears into her hair. "Will you be there?"

"Of course," said Althea. She too would be standing under the gazebo, also wearing a new dress, but instead of enjoying the spectacle of Seth dancing with his pregnant bride, she would be furtively watching the male guests, scrutinizing the way they watched Seth, straining to detect the narrowing of jealous eyes, an angry hand clutching a cocktail napkin. Looking for clues. Evidence. She wouldn't be able to report her findings to Max, but the Visible Man would be waiting for her back in her room at Sycamore Villas, lounging against his display stand. She would simply tell Rona that she wanted him, and Rona would give him to her.

She stood up. "Come on, mother of the groom," she said, pulling Rona to her feet. Rona stood before her, impotent, damp-haired, eyes downcast.

Althea had no idea what she was going to do until she did it. "Let's dance," she said. She placed one hand in the small of Rona's back and with the other she clasped Rona's hand. She'd forgotten she was so much taller than Rona.

"With you?" said Rona. "Now?"

"I'll teach you the swing." Althea began to hum "A String of Pearls" and guided Rona around the room, stepping left, right, back, pretending she knew what she was doing. She could still see the Arthur Murray sign that hung outside their kitchen window, she could still hear it buzzing—a neon outline of a dancing couple, the woman's yellow skirt blinking on and off, on and off.

She was leading perfectly, but Rona kept tripping. "Look at me!" said Althea. "I'm your dance partner, not your feet."

They ran into the rocking chair. "Ouch!" Rona yelped, but Althea kept them moving.

Rona wheezed with laughter. "We're clumsier than cows on ice," she said. Color had drained back into her face. "Is this really how you do it?"

"It's close enough," Althea said.

about the author

A GRADUATE of the Iowa Writers' Workshop, Elizabeth Stuckey-French has been awarded a James Michener Fellowship and her stories have appeared in *The Atlantic Monthly*, the *Gettysburg Review*, the *Southern Review*, and other literary magazines. She teaches fiction writing at Florida State University in Tallahassee, where she lives with her husband and two daughters.